"A LITERARY AND POLITICAL EVENT OF THE FIRST MAGNITUDE"

"Cannot fail to arouse bitterness and pain in the heart of the reader. A literary and political event of the first magnitude."

New Statesman

"Stark . . . the story of how one falsely accused convict and his fellow prisoners survived or perished in an arctic slave labor camp after the war."

Time

"Both as a political tract and as a literary work, it is in the DOCTOR ZHIVAGO category."

Washington Post

"Dramatic . . . outspoken . . . graphically detailed . . . a moving human record."

Library Journal

ONE DAY IN THE LIFE OF IVAN DENISOVICH

ALEXANDER SOLZHENITSYN

Translated by Max Hayward and Ronald Hingley
Introduction by Max Hayward and Leopold Labedz

BANTAM BOOKS

TORONTO • NEW YORK • LONDON • SYDNEY • AUCKLAND

*This low-priced Bantam Book
contains the complete text of
the original hard-cover edition.*
NOT ONE WORD HAS BEEN OMITTED.

ONE DAY IN THE LIFE OF IVAN DENISOVICH
*A Bantam Book / published by arrangement with
Praeger Publishers, Inc.*

PRINTING HISTORY
Praeger edition published January 1963
Bantam edition / January 1963
35 printings through June 1980
Bantam Windstone edition / June 1981
37th printing . September 1982
38th printing . . . . . May 1983
39th printing . . . August 1984

*Windstone and accompanying logo of a stylized W
are trademarks of Bantam Books, Inc.*

ISBN 0-553-24777-8

Published simultaneously in the United States and Canada

Bantam Books are published by Bantam Books, Inc. Its trademark, consisting of the words "Bantam Books" and the por-
trayal of a rooster, is Registered in U.S. Patent and Trademark
Office and in other countries. Marca Registrada. Bantam
Books, Inc., 666 Fifth Avenue, New York, New York 10103.

PRINTED IN THE UNITED STATES OF AMERICA

H   48 47 46 45 44 43 42 41 40

PUBLISHER'S NOTE*

THIS NEW EDITION of *One Day in the Life of Ivan Denisovich* includes the author's eloquent appeal for the abolishment of censorship in the Soviet Union. Mr. Solzhenitsyn wrote this letter to the Fourth National Congress of Soviet Writers in May, 1967.

Letter to the Fourth National Congress of Soviet Writers (In Lieu of a Speech)

TO THE PRESIDIUM and the delegates of the congress, to members of the Union of Soviet Writers, to the editors of literary newspapers and magazines:

I

The oppression, no longer tolerable, that our literature has been enduring from censorship for decades and that the Union of Writers cannot accept any further.

This censorship under the obscuring label of Glavlit [Soviet censorship agency], not provided for by the Constitution and therefore illegal and nowhere publicly labeled as such, is imposing a yoke on our literature and gives people who are unversed in literature arbitrary control over writers.

A survival of the Middle Ages, censorship manages in Methuselah-like fashion to drag out its existence almost to the 21st century. Of fleeting significance, it attempts to appropriate unto itself the role of unfleeting time of separating the good books from the bad.

Our writers are not supposed to have the right, they are not endowed with the right, to express their anticipatory judgments about the moral life of man and society, or to explain in their own way the social problems or the historical experience that has been so deeply felt in our country.

Works that might have expressed the mature thinking of the people, that might have timely and salutary influence on the realm of the spirit or on the development of a social conscience are prohibited or distorted by censorship on the basis of considerations that are petty, egotistic and, from the national point of view, shortsighted.

Outstanding manuscripts by young authors, as yet entirely unknown, are nowadays rejected by editors solely on the ground that they "will not pass."

Many union members and even delegates at this congress know how they themselves bowed to the pressure of censorship and made concessions in the structure and concept of their books, changing chapters, pages, paragraphs, sentences, giving them innocuous titles, only to see them finally in print, even if it meant distorting them irremediably.

We have one decisive factor here, the death of a troublesome writer, after which, sooner or later, he is returned to us, with an annotation "explaining his errors." For a long time, the name of Pasternak could not be pronounced out loud, but then he died, and his books appeared and his verse are even quoted at ceremonies.

Pushkin's words are really coming true: "They are capable of loving only the dead."

But tardy publication of books and "authorization" of names do not make up for either the social or the artistic losses suffered by our people from these monstrous delays, from the oppression of artistic conscience. (In fact there were writers in the 1920s, Pilnyak, Platonov and Mandelshtam, who called attention at a very early stage to the beginnings of the cult and the particular traits of Stalin's character; however, they were destroyed and silenced instead of being listened to.)

Literature cannot develop between the categories "permitted" —"not permitted"—"this you can and that you can't." Literature that is not the air of its contemporary society, that dares not pass on to society its pains and fears, that does not warn in time against threatening moral and social dangers, such literature does not deserve the name of literature; it is only a facade. Such literature loses the confidence of its own people, and its published works are used as waste paper instead of being read.

Our literature has lost the leading role it played at the end of the last century and the beginning of the present, and the brilliance of experimentation that distinguished it in the 1920s. To the entire world the literary life of our country now appears as something infinitely poorer, flatter and lower than it actually is, than it would appear if it were not restricted, hemmed in.

The losers are both our country, in world public opinion, and world literature itself. If the world had access to all the un-inhabited fruits of our literature, if it were enriched by our own spiritual experience, the whole artistic evolution of the world would move along in a different way, acquiring a new stability and attaining even a new artistic threshold.

I propose that the congress adopt a resolution that would demand and insure the abolition of all censorship, overt or hidden, of all fictional writing and release publishing houses from the obligation of obtaining authorization for the publication of every printed page.

II

The duties of the union toward its members:

These duties are not clearly formulated in the statutes of the Union of Soviet Writers (under "Protection of copyright" and "Measures for the protection of other rights of writers") , and it is sad to find that for a third of a century the union has defended neither the "other" rights nor even the copyright of persecuted writers.

Many writers were subjected during their lifetime to abuse and slander in the press and from rostrums without being given the physical possibility of replying. Moreover they have been exposed to violence and personal persecution (Bulgakov, Akhmatova, Tsvetayeva, Pasternak, Zoshchenko, Platonov, Aleksandr Grin, Vasily Grossman)

The Union of Writers not only did not make available its own publications for reply and justification, not only did not come out in defense of these writers, but through its leadership was always first among the persecutors.

Names that adorned our poetry of the 20th century found themselves on lists of those excluded from the union or not even admitted to the union in the first place.

The leadership of the union cowardly abandoned to their distress those for whom persecution ended in exile, camps and death (Pavel Vasilyev, Mandelshtam, Artem Vesely, Pilnyak, Babel, Tabidze, Zapolotsky and others).

The list must be cut off at "and others." We learned after the 20th congress of the party [on de-Stalinization in 1956] that there were more than 600 writers whom the union had obediently handed over to their fate in prisons and camps.

However, the roll is even longer, and its curled-up end cannot be read and will never be read by our eyes. It contains the names of young prose writers and poets whom we may have known only accidentally through personal meetings, whose talents were crushed in camps before being able to blossom, whose writings never got further than the offices of the state security service in the days of Yagoda, Yezhov, Beria and Abakumov [heads of the secret police under Stalin].

There is no historical necessity for the newly elected leadership of the union to share with preceding leaderships responsibility for the past.

I propose that paragraph 22 of the union statutes clearly formulate all the guarantees for the defense of union members who are subjected to slander and unjust persecutions so that past illegalities will not be repeated.

III

If the congress will not remain indifferent to what I have said, I also ask that it consider the interdictions and persecutions to which I myself have been subjected.

1. My novel "In the First Circle" was taken away from me almost two years ago by the state security people, and this has prevented it from being submitted to publishers. Instead, in my lifetime, against my will and even without my knowledge, this novel has been "published" in an unnatural "closed" edition for reading by a selected unidentified circle. My novel has become available to literary officials, but is being concealed from most writers. I have been unable to insure open discussion of the novel within writers associations and to prevent misuse and plagiarism.

2. Together with the novel, my literary archives dating back 15 and 20 years, things that were not intended for publication, were taken away from me. Now tendentious excerpts from these files have also been covertly "published" and are being circulated within the same circles. The play "Feast of the Victors,"

which I wrote down from memory in camp, where I figured under four serial numbers (at a time when, condemned to die by starvation, we were forgotten by society and no one outside the camps came out against repressions), this play, now left far behind, is being ascribed to me as my very latest work.

3. For three years now an irresponsible campaign of slander is being conducted against me, who fought all through the war as a battery commander and received military decorations. It is being said that I served time as a criminal, or surrendered to the enemy (I was never a prisoner of war), that I "betrayed" my country, "served the Germans." That is the interpretation now being put on the 11 years I spent in camps and exile for having criticized Stalin. This slander is being spread in secret instructions and meetings by people holding official positions. I vainly tried to stop the slander by appealing to the board of the Writers Union of the R.S.F.R. [Russian Republic] and to the press. The board did not even react, and not a single paper printed my reply to the slanderers. On the contrary, slander against me from rostrums has intensified and become more vicious within the last year, making use of distorted material from my confiscated files, and I have no way of replying.

4. My story "The Cancer Ward," the first part of which was approved for publication by the prose department of the Moscow writers organization, cannot be published either by chapters, rejected by five magazines, or in its entirety, rejected by Novy Mir, Zvezda and Prostor [literary journals].

5. The play "The Reindeer and the Little Hut," accepted in 1962 by the Theater Sovremennik [in Moscow], has thus far not received permission to be performed.

6. The screen play, "The Tanks Know the Truth," the stage play "The Light That Is in You," short stories, "The Right Hand," the series "Small Bits," cannot find either a producer or a publisher.

7. My stories published in Novy Mir have never been reprinted in book form, having been rejected everywhere —by the Soviet Writer Publishers, the State Literature Publishing House, the Ogonyok Library. They thus remain inaccessible to the general reading public.

8. I have also been prevented from having any other contacts with readers, public readings of my works—in November, 1966, 9 out of 11 scheduled meetings were canceled at the last moment—or readings over the radio. Even the simple act of giving

a manuscript away for "reading and copying" has now become a criminal act, and the ancient Russian scribes were permitted to do so.

My work has thus been finally smothered, gagged and slandered.

In view of such gross infringement on my copyright and "other" rights, will the fourth congress defend me, yes or no? It seems to me that the choice is also not without importance for the literary future of several delegates.

I am, of course, confident that I will fulfill my duty as a writer under all circumstances from the grave even more successfully and more unchallenged than in my lifetime. No one can bar the road to the truth, and to advance its cause I am prepared to accept even death. But, maybe, many lessons will finally teach us not to stop the writer's pen during his lifetime. At no time has this ennobled our history.

A. I. SOLZHENITSYN.

May 16, 1967.

Following are the names and identifications of Russian literary figures mentioned in Aleksandr I. Solzhenitsyn's letter calling for the abolition of censorship:

AKHMATOVA, Anna (1888-1966), poet, known for the intimate, personal character of her verse; denounced in 1946 in Stalinist literary purge.

BABEL, Isaak (1894-1941), prose writer, arrested in 1930's, died in forced labor camp. Author of "Red Cavalry," depicting violence of Russian Civil War.

BULGAKOV, Mikhail (1891-1940), novelist and playwright whose satirical works were implicit criticisms of Soviet regime. One of his plays "The Crimson Island" (1926), was direct attack on Soviet censorship. Some of his works have been republished and produced within last year.

BUNIN, Ivan (1870-1953), prose writer, emigrated from Soviet Union in 1921, won Nobel Prize in 1933. Despite hostility to Soviet regime, a one-volume selection of his works was published in Moscow after his death, followed by five volumes of his collected works.

DOSTOYEVSKY, Fyodor (1821-81), novelist. Spent four years in Siberian exile because of association in the 1840's with the Petrashevsky Circle, a discussion society of utopian socialists, Depicted his experiences in "Memoirs from the House of the Dead."

GRIN, Aleksandr (1880-1932), popular author of fantastic tales, found by official Soviet critics to be out of line with Soviet era.

GROSSMAN, Vasily (1905-1964), novelist whose war novel "For the Just Cause" (1952), about battle of Stalingrad, was officially criticized in last years of Stalin era for not being sufficiently party-oriented.

GUMILEV, Nikolai (1886-1921), poet of Acmeist school, noted for clarity and concreteness of imagery. He was executed on charges of anti-Soviet plotting.

KLYUYEV, Nikolai (1887-1937), peasant poet whose early enthusiasm for Soviet system gave way to disillusionment. Arrested in 1933 and died in a prison camp.

MANDELSHTAM, Osip (1891-1942), poet, noted for coldly detached, sophisticated, sometimes obscure verse. Arrested in early 1930's, allowed to return to Moscow, banished again to Siberia, where he died.

MAYAKOVSKY, Vladimir (1893-1930), leading poet of early Soviet period. Suicide attributed by some to disillusionment with Soviet life.

PASTERNAK, Boris (1890-1960), lyric poet, translator, and author of novel, "Doctor Zhivago," which was smuggled abroad and won him Nobel Prize in 1958. Died in disgrace. After his death, his poetry was republished.

PILNYAK, Boris (1894-1937), novelist criticized in the late 1920's for unorthodox works and stylistic and typographical experimentation. Disappeared in the purges.

PLATONOV, Andrei (1896-1951), short-story writer, member of group that opposed proletarian literature in 1920's. Stories have folklore backgrounds, heroes are concerned with religious and moral issues. Protested depersonalization of man by machine.

REMIZOV, Aleksei (1877-1957), prose writer, left Soviet Union in 1921 and died in Paris. Works have whimsical, grotesque or religious overtones.

TABIDZE, Titsian (1895-1937), Georgian poet, translated by Pasternak; disappeared in Stalinist purges.

TSVETAYEVA, Marina (1894-1941), poet known for spontaneous, passionate verses, left Soviet Union in 1921, returned in 1939 and committed suicide in 1941.

VESELY, Artem (1899-1939), prose writer, disciple of Pilnyak, disappeared in Stalinist purges. Has been quietly rehabilitated through the reissue of selected writings.

VASILYEV, Pavel (1910-37), poet, former seaman and Siberian gold miner, perished in Stalinist purges. Work reflected an artist's problems in overcoming old traditions and adjusting to new society.

VOLOSHIN, Maximilian (1878-1932), Symbolist poet who openly opposed the revolution but remained in Soviet Union, living in seclusion in Crimea as a "spiritual émigré."

YESENIN, Sergei (1895-1925), leading early poet of Soviet period, of peasant background, opposed emphasis on industrialization, known for a widely publicized, rowdy personal life. A suicide.

ZAMYATIN, Yevgeny (1884-1937), prose writer, hostile to Soviet regime; his stories warned of coercion and uniformity in a Communist society. Silenced after late 1920's, he was permitted to emigrate in 1932 and died in Paris.

ZABOLOTSKY, Nikolai (1903-58), poet arrested in Stalinist purges of late 1930's, survived eight years of imprisonment and was rehabilitated.

ZOSHCHENKO, Mikail (1895-1946), author of outspoken satirical short stories. Denounced with Anna Akhmatova in 1946 during crackdown on arts.

INTRODUCTION

ALEXANDER SOLZHENITSYN'S *One Day in the Life of Ivan Denisovich* is beyond doubt the most startling work ever to have been published in the Soviet Union. Apart from being a literary masterpiece, it is a revolutionary document that will affect the climate of life inside the Soviet Union. It is a pitiless and relentlessly told tale of forced labor camps under Stalin.

Solzhenitsyn has laid bare a whole new world. For a quarter of a century, the vast concentration camp system created by Stalin was, directly or indirectly, part of the daily life of all Soviet citizens. There was hardly a family that did not have a son, a husband, a brother, or some other relative in a camp, and the truth of what Solzhenitsyn says has long been known, but not always believed, outside the Soviet Union.

But Solzhenitsyn's book, because of its supreme artistic quality, creates a greater impression of horror and revulsion than anything ever published abroad by even the most embittered victims of Soviet camps.

For several years now, it has been possible to mention the existence of concentration camps under Stalin in Soviet literature, and, indeed, the figure of the returned prisoner has become a commonplace, but what life was actually like in this man-made hell has never before been revealed in print to Soviet readers.

The blanket of silence over the prison-camp universe was as thick as the snow over the world's greatest land mass, stretching from the Kola Peninsula to Magadan, from Vorkuta to Kolyma.

In their struggle to rise from the depths of degradation into which they were plunged by Stalin, Soviet writers had to come to terms sooner or later with his betrayal of that deep humanity which once made Russian literature so great in the eyes of the world. It has fallen to Alexander Solzhenitsyn to restore the literary and human values of the past. It is fitting that he has chosen to do this by ruthlessly exposing the shameful institution that was at once the instrument and the embodiment of an utterly despicable tyranny. Solzhenitsyn has thereby eased the tormented conscience of those innumerable Russians who for so long have had to live in silence with the knowledge of this shame. As Alexander Tvardovsky says in his preface: "The effect of this novel, which is so unusual for its honesty and harrowing truth, is to unburden our minds of things thus far unspoken, but which had to be said. It thereby strengthens and ennobles us." The power of the novel is such that we too can share this feeling.

The conscience of the nation could scarcely be satisfied by the smug formula, sickening in its hypocrisy, by which, since the years of the Twentieth Congress of the CPSU, the "mistakes" of Stalin were ascribed to "certain phenomena associated with the personality cult." Solzhenitsyn's novel transcends this convention.

In other ways, too, Solzhenitsyn goes far beyond the bounds of what had hitherto been permissible in public discussions about the past. He shows that the camps were not an isolated feature in an otherwise admirable society—the unfortunate result of a temporary "infringement of socialist legality"—but that they were, in fact, microcosms of that society as a whole. The novel draws an implicit parallel between life "inside" and "outside" the camp: A day in the life of an ordinary Soviet citizen had much in common with that of his unfortunate fellow countrymen behind barbed wire. We now see that on both sides of the fence it was the same story of material and spiritual squalor, corruption, frustration, and terror.

By choosing as the hero of his tale a very ordinary working man, Solzhenitsyn has broken another convention. Ivan Denisovich is no standard hero of labor bearing aloft the banner of triumphant socialism and striding confidently into the glorious Communist future. He is a humble, utterly bewildered plain man who wants nothing more than to live out a normal working life as best he can. He struggles pathetically to maintain his honesty, self-respect, and pride in a hopeless battle with mysterious forces that seem determined—for reasons beyond his ken—to destroy his human dignity, to deny him his right to love his country, and to render meaningless the work of his hands. Up to now we have heard only about more exalted victims of "the period of the personality cult." In the campaign of rehabilitation initiated by the heirs to Stalin's power, the emphasis has been on "honest Communists unjustly sentenced." Now, for the first time, we learn from Solzhenitsyn of the way in which millions of nameless people paid with their freedom and with life itself for the "construction of socialism."

Solzhenitsyn has destroyed for all time the web of lies that has surrounded Soviet concentration camps for more than three decades—not to mention the myths propagated with such confidence and with such arrogance, all evidence to the contrary, by the self-appointed "friends of the Soviet Union," who now stand revealed as traitors to the true Russia and to all humanity. On their conscience be it.

It would be wrong, however, to consider Solzhenitsyn's novel only in crassly historical and political terms. Like all great works of art, it is outside place and time. In showing one man, in one particular time and place, in the most sordid setting imaginable, Solzhenitsyn has succeeded in strengthening our faith in the ultimate victory of civilized values over evil. His novel is a morality play in which the carpenter Ivan Denisovich Shukhov is Everyman.

New York   MAX HAYWARD
January, 1963   LEOPOLD LABEDZ

EXPLANATORY NOTES

THE following notes refer to words asterisked in the text, in the order in which they appear.

"Free" workers (*Volnye*) —The term used by the prisoners about the people "outside" (*navole*). These "free" workers employed on construction sites in the vicinity of Soviet concentration camps were mostly former prisoners themselves who, after serving their sentences, either had no home to go back to or were not allowed by the authorities to return to their former places of residence.

Western Ukrainian—A native of that Ukrainian territory which until World War II belonged to Poland and was subsequently annexed by the Soviet Union. The implication of the passage is that the people in this region still had not lost some of the manners of non-Soviet society.

Ust-Izhma—One of the many camps on the river Pechora, which flows into the Barents Sea. In these camps, the prisoners were employed mostly in cutting timber.

"Special" camp (*Osoblager*) —Camps with a particularly harsh regime.

Volkovoy—A name derived from *volk,* meaning "wolf."

Article 58—The notorious article of the Soviet Criminal Code that covers a wide range of "anti-Soviet" offenses—espionage, sabotage, propaganda against the regime—and was interpreted to cover the activities of any "socially dangerous elements." Under Stalin, it was applied indiscriminately and automatically to untold numbers of people (like Shukhov in this novel) on mere suspicion of disloyalty or disaffection.

Old Believers (*Staroobryadtsy*) —Schismatics of the Russian Orthodox Church who refused to accept certain reforms introduced by the Patriarch Nikon in the seventeenth century. They were persecuted both under the Czars and under the Soviets.

Bendera—Stepan Bendera, the leader of the Western Ukrainian nationalist partisans who at first collaborated with the Germans against the Soviets during the war, but then became disillusioned with the Germans and continued guerrilla warfare on Soviet territory until about 1950. Bendera was assassinated by Soviet agents in Germany in October, 1959.

"Goner" (*Dokhodyaga*) —Camp slang for a prisoner who was so exhausted by work and wasted by disease that he had little time left to live.

Oprichniki—Ivan the Terrible's janizaries, who in the sixteenth century were used to crush all opposition to the Czar.

"How are you serving?" . . . "I serve the working people."—A standard form of address between officers and men in the Soviet Army.

"Kirov business"—Sergei Kirov, a member of the Politburo and Party boss of Leningrad. His assassination there in 1934, probably engineered by Stalin himself, provided the excuse for mass arrests and the liquidation of real and imagined political opponents that culminated in the Great Purge of 1936-38.

Zavadsky—Yuri Zavadsky, a prominent Soviet stage producer associated with the Moscow Art Theater, the Theater of the Red Army, and the Theater of the Moscow City Soviet.

TRANSLATORS' NOTE

SOLZHENITSYN's novel presents unique problems of translation. Not only the dialogue, but the narrative is written in a peculiar mixture of concentration camp slang and the language of a Russian peasant. The translators have sought to render something of the flavor of this by using the uneducated speech forms of American English. A further difficulty has been the author's liberal use of common Russian obscenities. These have never before appeared in print in the Soviet Union, and even here they are rendered in a slightly disguised form. The translators of this version have thought it best to ignore the prudish conventions of Soviet publishing and spell out the English equivalents in full.

The translators wish to thank Mr. Vladimir Yurasov for his help in elucidating certain obscure words and phrases. They are also greatly indebted to Jean Steinberg, Phyllis Freeman, and Arnold Dolin for their invaluable and devoted editorial assistance.

INSTEAD OF A FOREWORD*

THE SUBJECT MATTER of Alexander Solzhenitsyn's novel is unusual in Soviet literature. It echoes the unhealthy phenomena in our life associated with the period of the personality cult, now exposed and rejected by the Party. Although these events are so recent in point of time, they seem very remote to us. But whatever the past was like, we in the present must not be indifferent to it. Only by going into its consequences fully, courageously, and truthfully can we guarantee a complete and irrevocable break with all those things that cast a shadow over the past. This is what N. S. Khrushchev meant when he said in his memorable concluding address at the Twenty-second Congress: "It is our duty to go carefully into all aspects of all matters connected with the abuse of power. In time we must die, for we are all mortal, but as long as we go on working we can and must clarify many things and tell the truth to the Party and the people. . . . This must be done to prevent such things from happening in the future."

One Day in the Life of Ivan Denisovich is not a book of memoirs in the ordinary sense of the word. It does not consist merely of notes on the author's personal experiences and his memories of them, although only personal experience could have given the novel such an authentic quality. It is a work of art. And it is the way in which the raw material is handled that gives it its outstanding value as a testimony and makes it an artistic document, the possibility of which had hitherto seemed unlikely on the basis of "concrete material."

In Solzhenitsyn the reader will not find an exhaustive account of that historical period marked in particular by the year 1937, so bitter in all our memories. The theme of *One Day* is inevitably limited by the time and place of the action and by the boundaries of the world to which the hero was confined. One day of Ivan Denisovich Shukhov, a prisoner in a forced labor camp, as described by Alexander Solzhenitsyn (this is the author's first appearance in print) unfolds as a picture of exceptional vividness and truthfulness about the nature of man. It is this above all that gives the work its unique impact. The reader

* TRANSLATORS' NOTE: This statement by the Editor in Chief of *Novy Mir* appeared as a preface to the novel in the November, 1962, issue of that journal.

could easily imagine many of the people shown here in these tragic circumstances as fighting at the front or working on post-war reconstruction. They are the same sort of people, but they have been exposed by fate to a cruel ordeal—not only physical but moral.

The author of this novel does not go out of his way to emphasize the arbitrary brutality which was a consequence of the breakdown of Soviet legality. He has taken a very ordinary day —from reveille to lights out—in the life of a prisoner. But this ordinary day cannot fail to fill the reader's heart with bitterness and pain at the fate of these people who come to life before his eyes and seem to close to him in the pages of this book. The author's greatest achievement, however, is that this bitterness and pain do not convey a feeling of utter despair. On the contrary. The effect of this novel, which is so unusual for its honesty and harrowing truth, is to unburden our minds of things thus far unspoken, but which had to be said. It thereby strengthens and ennobles us.

This stark tale shows once again that today there is no aspect of our life that cannot be dealt with and faithfully described in Soviet literature. Now it is only a question of how much talent the writer brings to it. There is another very simple lesson to be learned from this novel. If the theme of a work is truly significant, if it is faithful to the great truths of life, and if it is deeply human in its presentation of even the most painful subjects, then it cannot help find the appropriate form of expression. The style of *One Day* is vivid and original in its unpretentiousness and down-to-earth simplicity. It is quite unself-conscious and thereby gains great inner strength and dignity.

I do not want to anticipate readers' judgments of this short work, but I myself have not the slightest doubt that it marks the appearance on the literary scene of a new, original, and mature talent.

It may well be that the author's use—however sparing and to the point—of certain words and expressions typical of the setting in which the hero lived and worked may offend a particularly fastidious taste. But all in all, *One Day* is a work for which one has such a feeling of gratitude to the author that one's greatest wish is that this gratitude be shared by other readers.

ALEXANDER TVARDOVSKY

R EVEILLE was sounded, as always, at 5 A.M.—a
hammer pounding on a rail outside camp HQ.
The ringing noise came faintly on and off
through the windowpanes covered with ice more
than an inch thick, and died away fast. It was
cold and the warder didn't feel like going on
banging.

The sound stopped and it was pitch black on the
other side of the window, just like in the middle
of the night when Shukhov had to get up to go to
the latrine, only now three yellow beams fell on the
window—from two lights on the perimeter and one
inside the camp.

He didn't know why but nobody'd come to open
up the barracks. And you couldn't hear the orderlies
hoisting the latrine tank on the poles to carry it out.

Shukhov never slept through reveille but always
got up at once. That gave him about an hour and a
half to himself before the morning roll call, a time
when anyone who knew what was what in the camps

could always scrounge a little something on the side. He could sew someone a cover for his mittens out of a piece of old lining. He could bring one of the big gang bosses his dry felt boots while he was still in his bunk, to save him the trouble of hanging around the pile of boots in his bare feet and trying to find his own. Or he could run around to one of the supply rooms where there might be a little job, sweeping or carrying something. Or he could go to the mess hall to pick up bowls from the tables and take piles of them to the dishwashers. That was another way of getting food, but there were always too many other people with the same idea. And the worst thing was that if there was something left in a bowl you started to lick it. You couldn't help it. And Shukhov could still hear the words of his first gang boss, Kuzyomin—an old camp hand who'd already been inside for twelve years in 1943. Once, by a fire in a forest clearing, he'd said to a new batch of men just brought in from the front:

"It's the law of the jungle here, fellows. But even here you can live. The first to go is the guy who licks out bowls, puts his faith in the infirmary, or squeals to the screws."

He was dead right about this—though it didn't always work out that way with the fellows who squealed to the screws. They knew how to look after themselves. They got away with it and it was the other guys who suffered.

Shukhov always got up at reveille, but today he didn't. He'd been feeling lousy since the night before—with aches and pains and the shivers, and he just couldn't manage to keep warm that night. In his sleep he'd felt very sick and then again a little better. All the time he dreaded the morning.

But the morning came, as it always did.

Anyway, how could anyone get warm here, what with the ice piled up on the window and a white cobweb of frost running along the whole barracks where the walls joined the ceiling? And a hell of a barracks it was.

Shukhov stayed in bed. He was lying on the top bunk, with his blanket and overcoat over his head and both his feet tucked in the sleeve of his jacket. He couldn't see anything, but he could tell by the sounds what was going on in the barracks and in his own part of it. He could hear the orderlies tramping down the corridor with one of the twenty-gallon latrine tanks. This was supposed to be light work for people on the sick list—but it was no joke carrying the thing out without spilling it! Then someone from Gang 75 dumped a pile of felt boots from the drying room on the floor. And now someone from his gang did the same (it was also their turn to use the drying room today). The gang boss and his assistant quickly put on their boots, and their bunk creaked. The assistant gang boss would now go and get the bread rations. And then the boss would take off

3

for the Production Planning Section (PPS) at HQ.

But, Shukhov remembered, this wasn't just the same old daily visit to the PPS clerks. Today was the big day for them. They'd heard a lot of talk of switching their gang—104—from putting up workshops to a new job, building a new "Socialist Community Development." But so far it was nothing more than bare fields covered with snowdrifts, and before anything could be done there, holes had to be dug, posts put in, and barbed wire put up—by the prisoners for the prisoners, so they couldn't get out. And then they could start building.

You could bet your life that for a month there'd be no place where you could get warm—not even a hole in the ground. And you couldn't make a fire—what could you use for fuel? So your only hope was to work like hell.

The gang boss was worried and was going to try to fix things, try to palm the job off on some other gang, one that was a little slower on the uptake. Of course you couldn't go empty-handed. It would take a pound of fatback for the chief clerk. Or even two.

Maybe Shukhov would try to get himself on the sick list so he could have a day off. There was no harm in trying. His whole body was one big ache.

Then he wondered—which warder was on duty today?

He remembered that it was Big Ivan, a tall, scrawny sergeant with black eyes. The first time you saw him he scared the pants off you, but when you got to know him he was the easiest of all the duty warders—wouldn't put you in the can or drag you off to the disciplinary officer. So Shukhov could stay put till it was time for Barracks 9 to go to the mess hall.

The bunk rocked and shook as two men got up together—on the top Shukhov's neighbor, the Baptist Alyoshka, and down below Buynovsky, who'd been a captain in the navy.

When they'd carried out the two latrine tanks, the orderlies started quarreling about who'd go to get the hot water. They went on and on like two old women. The electric welder from Gang 20 barked at them:

"Hey, you old bastards!" And he threw a boot at them. "I'll make you shut up."

The boot thudded against a post. The orderlies shut up.

The assistant boss of the gang next to them grumbled in a low voice.

"Vasili Fyodorovich! The bastards pulled a fast one on me in the supply room. We always get four two-pound loaves, but today we only got three. Someone'll have to get the short end."

He spoke quietly, but of course the whole gang heard him and they all held their breath. Who was going to be shortchanged on rations this evening?

5

Shukhov stayed where he was, on the hard-packed sawdust of his mattress. If only it was one thing or another—either a high fever or an end to the pain. But this way he didn't know where he was.

While the Baptist was whispering his prayers, the Captain came back from the latrine and said to no one in particular, but sort of gloating:

"Brace yourselves, men! It's at least twenty below."

Shukhov made up his mind to go to the infirmary.

And then some strong hand stripped his jacket and blanket off him. Shukhov jerked his quilted overcoat off his face and raised himself up a bit. Below him, his head level with the top of the bunk, stood the Thin Tartar.

So this bastard had come on duty and sneaked up on them.

"S-854!" the Tartar read from the white patch on the back of the black coat. "Three days in the can with work as usual."

The minute they heard his funny muffled voice everyone in the entire barracks—which was pretty dark (not all the lights were on) and where two hundred men slept in fifty bug-ridden bunks—came to life all of a sudden. Those who hadn't yet gotten up began to dress in a hurry.

"But what for, Comrade Warder?" Shukhov asked, and he made his voice sound more pitiful than he really felt.

6

The can was only half as bad if you were given normal work. You got hot food and there was no time to brood. Not being let out to work—that was real punishment.

"Why weren't you up yet? Let's go to the Commandant's office," the Tartar drawled—he and Shukhov and everyone else knew what he was getting the can for.

There was a blank look on the Tartar's hairless, crumpled face. He turned around and looked for somebody else to pick on, but everyone—whether in the dark or under a light, whether on a bottom bunk or a top one—was shoving his legs into the black, padded trousers with numbers on the left knee. Or they were already dressed and were wrapping themselves up and hurrying for the door to wait outside till the Tartar left.

If Shukhov had been sent to the can for something he deserved he wouldn't have been so upset. What made him mad was that he was always one of the first to get up. But there wasn't a chance of getting out of it with the Tartar. So he went on asking to be let off just for the hell of it, but meantime pulled on his padded trousers (they too had a worn, dirty piece of cloth sewed above the left knee, with the number S-854 painted on it in black and already faded), put on his jacket (this had two numbers, one on the chest and one on the back), took his boots from the pile on the floor, put on his cap (with the same num-

7

ber in front), and went out after the Tartar.

The whole Gang 104 saw Shukhov being taken off, but no one said a word. It wouldn't help, and what could you say? The gang boss might have stood up for him, but he'd left already. And Shukhov himself said nothing to anyone. He didn't want to aggravate the Tartar. They'd keep his breakfast for him and didn't have to be told.

The two of them went out.

It was freezing cold, with a fog that caught your breath. Two large searchlights were crisscrossing over the compound from the watchtowers at the far corners. The lights on the perimeter and the lights inside the camp were on full force. There were so many of them that they blotted out the stars.

With their felt boots crunching on the snow, prisoners were rushing past on their business—to the latrines, to the supply rooms, to the package room, or to the kitchen to get their groats cooked. Their shoulders were hunched and their coats buttoned up, and they all felt cold, not so much because of the freezing weather as because they knew they'd have to be out in it all day. But the Tartar in his old overcoat with shabby blue tabs walked steadily on and the cold didn't seem to bother him at all.

They went past the high wooden fence around the punishment block (the stone prison inside the camp), past the barbed-wire fence that guarded the bakery from the prisoners, past the corner of the HQ where a length of frost-covered rail was fastened to a post with heavy wire, and past another post where —in a sheltered spot to keep the readings from being too low—the thermometer hung, caked over with ice. Shukhov gave a hopeful sidelong glance at the milk-white tube. If it went down to forty-two below zero they weren't supposed to be marched out to work. But today the thermometer wasn't pushing forty or anything like it.

They went into HQ—straight into the warders' room. There it turned out—as Shukhov had already had a hunch on the way—that they never meant to put him in the can but simply that the floor in the warders' room needed scrubbing. Sure enough, the Tartar now told Shukhov that he was letting him off and ordered him to mop the floor.

Mopping the floor in the warders' room was the job of a special prisoner—the HQ orderly, who never worked outside the camp. But a long time ago he'd set himself up in HQ and now had a free run of the rooms where the Major, the disciplinary officer, and the security chief worked. He waited on them all the time and sometimes got to hear things even the warders didn't know. And for some time he'd figured that to scrub floors for ordinary warders was a little beneath him. They called for him once or twice, then got wise and began pulling in ordinary prisoners to do the job.

The stove in the warders' room was blazing away. A couple of warders who'd undressed down to their dirty shirts were playing checkers, and a third who'd left on his belted sheepskin coat and felt boots was sleeping on a narrow bench. There was a bucket and rag in the corner.

Shukhov was real pleased and thanked the Tartar for letting him off:

"Thank you, Comrade Warder. I'll never get up late again."

The rule here was simple—finish your job and get out. Now that Shukhov had been given some work, his pains seemed to have stopped. He took the bucket and went to the well without his mittens, which he'd forgotten and left under his pillow in the rush.

The gang bosses reporting at the PPS had formed a small group near the post, and one of the younger ones, who was once a Hero of the Soviet Union, climbed up and wiped the thermometer.

The others were shouting up to him: "Don't breathe on it or it'll go up."

"Go up . . . the hell it will . . . it won't make a fucking bit of difference anyway."

Tyurin—the boss of Shukhov's work gang—was not there. Shukhov put down the bucket and dug his hands into his sleeves. He wanted to see what was going on.

The fellow up the post said in a hoarse voice: "Seventeen and a half below—shit!"

And after another look just to make sure, he jumped down.

"Anyway, it's always wrong—it's a damned liar," someone said. "They'd never put in one that works here."

The gang bosses scattered. Shukhov ran to the well. Under the flaps of his cap, which he'd lowered but hadn't tied, his ears ached with the cold.

The top of the well was covered by a thick crust of ice so that the bucket would hardly go through the hole. And the rope was stiff as a board.

Shukhov's hands were frozen, so when he got back to the warders' room with the steaming bucket he shoved them in the water. He felt warmer.

The Tartar had gone, but four of the warders were there quarreling. They'd quit playing checkers or sleeping and they were arguing about how much millet they'd get in January. (There was a shortage of food in the local "free" workers'* settlement, and though ration cards had gone out a long time ago, the warders could still buy some foodstuffs at a cut rate the locals couldn't get.)

"Shut the door, you shithead! It's cold," one of them shouted.

It wasn't a good idea to get your felt boots wet in the morning. You didn't have anything extra to change into, even if you could run back to your barracks. During his eight years inside, Shukhov had seen all kinds of ups and downs in the footwear situation. There'd been times when they'd gone around all winter without any felt boots at all, times when they hadn't even seen ordinary boots but only shoes made of birch bark or shoes of the "Chelyabinsk Tractor Factory model" (that is, made of strips of tires that left the marks of the tread behind them). Now the boot situation had begun to look up. In October—this because he'd once managed to wangle himself a trip to the stores with the number-two man in his gang—Shukhov had gotten a pair of sturdy boots with good strong toes that were roomy enough inside for two thicknesses of warm foot-cloths. For a week he was on top of the world and went around knocking his new heels together with joy. Then felt boots were issued in December and life was great. You didn't want to die. Then some swine in the book-keeping department put a bug in the Commandant's ear: "Let 'em have the felt boots, but make 'em hand in the others. It's not right for a prisoner to have two pairs at the same time." So Shukhov had to choose whether he'd get through the whole winter in the new boots or take the felt boots—right through the spring thaws—and hand in the new ones. He'd treated them with loving care, he rubbed them with grease to make the leather soft, those lovely new boots. During the whole eight years, nothing had hit him more than having to turn in those boots. They'd been dumped with all the others in one heap, and he'd never find them again in the spring.

Now Shukhov had an idea. He quickly kicked off his felt boots, stood them in a corner, threw the footcloths on top of them (the spoon he always kept in one boot clattered onto the floor—even in the rush to leave the barracks, he hadn't forgotten it), and dropped to the floor in his bare feet and started sloshing water right under the warders' boots.

"Take it easy, you bastard!" one of them said, seeing what Shukhov was up to, and he lifted up his feet.

. . . "What do you mean, rice? That's on a different quota and there's just no comparison." . . .

"Why are you using all that water, stupid? That's no way to wash a floor."

"There's no other way, Comrade Warder! The dirt's worked right into it."

"Didn't you ever see your old lady wash the floor, stupid?"

Shukhov straightened up and held the dripping rag in his hand. He gave an innocent smile which showed that some of his teeth were missing—they'd been thinned out by scurvy at Ust-Izhma in 1943, a time when he thought he was on his last legs. He was really far gone. He had the runs, with bleeding, and his insides were so worn out he couldn't keep anything down. But now all that was left from those days was his funny way of talking.

"They took me away from her in 1941, Comrade

Warder. I don't even remember what she was like."

"Just look at how they mop. . . . The bastards can't do anything and don't want to either. They're not worth the bread we give 'em. They ought to get shit instead."

"Anyway, why mop the fucking thing every day? It makes the place damp all the time. Now, 854, listen here. Just wipe it over a little so it's not too wet and get the hell out of here."

. . . "Rice! You can't compare millet and rice!" . . .

Shukhov quickly finished up the job. There's work and work. It's like the two ends of a stick. If you're working for human beings, then do a real job of it, but if you work for dopes, then you just go through the motions. Otherwise they'd all have kicked the bucket long ago. That was for sure.

Shukhov went over the floorboards, leaving no dry patches, threw his rag behind the stove without wringing it out, pulled on his boots, splashed the water out of his pail onto the path used by the top brass, and cut across to the mess hall, past the bathhouse and the dark, cold recreation hall.

He also had to make it to the hospital block—he was aching all over again. Then he had to keep out of sight of the warders in front of the mess hall. The Commandant had given strict orders to pick up any stray prisoners and put them in the cells.

Today (this didn't often happen) there wasn't a

big crowd lined up in front of the mess hall. So he went straight in.

It was like a steam bath inside—what with the frosty air coming in through the doors and the steam from the thin camp gruel. The men were sitting at tables or crowding in the spaces between them, waiting for places. Shouting their way through the mob, two or three prisoners from each gang were carrying bowls of gruel and mush on wooden trays and looking for a place for them on the tables. And even so, they don't hear you, the dopes, they bump into your tray and you spill the stuff! And then you let them have it in the neck with your free hand! That's how to do it. That'll teach them to get in the way looking out for leftovers.

On the other side of the table there was a young fellow who was crossing himself before he started to eat. Must have been a Western Ukrainian* and new to the place. The Russians didn't even remember which hand you cross yourself with.

It was cold sitting in the mess hall and most of the men ate with their caps on, but without hurrying, chasing bits of rotten fish among the cabbage leaves and spitting the bones out on the table. When there was a whole pile of them, someone would sweep them off before the next gang came, and they were ground underfoot on the floor.

Spitting the bones out on the floor was thought bad manners.

In the middle of the mess hall there were two rows of what you might call pillars or supports. Fetyukov, another fellow from the same gang, was sitting by one of them and guarding Shukhov's breakfast. He didn't count for much in the gang—even less than Shukhov. To look at them, the gang was all the same —the same black overcoats and numbers—but underneath they were all different. You couldn't ask the Captain to guard your bowl, and there were jobs even Shukhov wouldn't do—jobs that were beneath him.

Fetyukov spotted Shukhov and gave up his seat with a sigh.

"It's all cold now. I was going to eat it for you—I thought you were in the cooler."

He didn't wait around. He knew that Shukhov wouldn't leave him any. He'd polish off both bowls himself.

Shukhov pulled his spoon out of his boot. He was very fond of this spoon, which had gone with him all over the North. He'd made it himself from aluminum wire and cast it in sand. And he'd scratched on it: "Ust-Izhma, 1944."*

Then Shukhov took his cap off his shaved head—however cold it was, he would never eat with it on. He stirred up the cold gruel and took a quick look to see what was in his bowl. It was the usual thing. It hadn't been ladled from the top of the caldron, but it wasn't the stuff from the bottom either. He wouldn't put it past Fetyukov to pinch a potato from it.

The only good thing about camp gruel was it was usually hot, but what Shukhov had was now quite cold. Even so, he ate it slow and careful like he always did. Mustn't hurry now, even if the roof caught fire. Apart from sleeping, the prisoners' time was their own only for ten minutes at breakfast, five minutes at the noon break, and another five minutes at supper.

The gruel didn't change from one day to the next. It depended on what vegetables they'd stored for winter. The year before they'd only stocked up with salted carrots, so there was nothing but carrots in the gruel from September to June. And now it was cabbage. The camp was fed best in June, when they ran out of vegetables and started using groats instead. The worst time was July, when they put shredded nettles in the caldron.

The fish was mostly bones. The flesh was boiled off except for bits on the tails and the heads. Not leaving a single scale or speck of flesh on the skeleton, Shukhov crunched and sucked the bones and spit them out on the table. He didn't leave anything—not even the gills or the tail. He ate the eyes too when they were still in place, but when they'd come off and were floating around in the bowl on their own he didn't eat them. The others laughed at him for this.

Shukhov made a kind of saving today. He hadn't been back to his barracks to collect his bread ration, and now he was eating without it. Bread—well, you could always eat that by itself, and he'd feel less hungry later on.

The second course was a mush out of *magara*. It was one solid lump, and Shukhov broke it off in pieces. When it was hot—never mind when it was cold—it had no taste and didn't fill you. It was nothing but grass that looked like millet. They'd gotten the bright idea of serving it instead of groats. It came from the Chinese, they said. They got ten ounces of it and that was that. It wasn't the real thing, but it passed for mush.

He licked his spoon, pushed it back in his boot, put on his cap, and went to the hospital block.

The sky was as dark as ever, and the stars were blotted out by the camp lights. And the two search-lights were cutting broad swathes through the compound. At the time they set up the camp—it was a "Special" one*—the guards still had a lot of flares. If the electricity failed, they'd send a shower of rockets over the compound—white, green, and red—just like at the front. Then they stopped using them. Maybe they thought it was too expensive.

It was just as dark as it was at reveille. But from this, that and the other an old hand could see that roll call would soon be sounded. Clubfoot's assistant

(Clubfoot was a mess-hall orderly who kept an assistant out of his own pocket) had gone to summon Barracks 6 to breakfast. Number 6 was for invalids, men who couldn't work off the compound. An old artist with a little beard trotted over to the Culture and Education Section (CES) to get paint and a brush to paint number tags for prison uniforms. Once more the Tartar dashed across the yard toward HQ. There weren't many people around. They'd all gone under cover and were warming themselves these last sweet minutes.

Shukhov ducked behind the corner of a hut to get out of the Tartar's way. If he caught him a second time he'd screw him good. Anyway, you had to keep your eyes open all the time. You had to be careful the warders didn't see you alone, but only in a crowd. They were always on the lookout for someone to do a job or to have someone to pick on if they were in a lousy mood. They'd put out a standing order in the camp that you had to take your cap off at a distance of five paces when you saw a warder, and keep it off till you were two paces past him. Some of the warders wandered around with their eyes shut and just didn't care, but others got a kick out of it. The number of guys that had been put in the can just on this! No thank you. Better to wait around the corner.

The Tartar went by. And Shukhov was just about to go on to the hospital when he suddenly remembered that the Latvian in Barracks 7 had told him to come this morning before roll call to buy a couple of mugs of tobacco. But Shukhov was so busy it had gone clean out of his head. The big Latvian had gotten a package from home the evening before, and maybe by tomorrow there wouldn't be any left. It might be a month before there'd be another package. And his tobacco was good. It had the right strength and it smelled good and it was sort of brownish.

Shukhov felt bothered and stopped dead. Should he look in at Number 7? But he was near the hospital, so he went on up to the steps. The snow crunched under his feet.

The corridor in the hospital was so clean—it always was—that he was scared to walk along it. The walls were painted a shiny white, and the furniture was all white as well.

But the office doors were shut. The doctors must still be in bed. One of the medics—a young fellow by the name of Nikolay Vdovushkin—was sitting in the orderlies' room at a nice clean desk and he was wearing a nice clean white coat. He was writing something.

There was no one else around.

Shukhov took off his hat, as though this was one of the higher-ups, and in the good old camp fashion, looking at things you weren't supposed to see, he couldn't help noticing that Vdovushkin was writing in neat, straight lines, starting each line right under the one before with a capital letter and leaving a little room at the side. Shukhov saw at once, of course, that this wasn't work but some stuff of his own and none of Shukhov's business.

"Listen, Nikolay Semyonovich, I'm feeling kind of sick," he said, with a hangdog look, as if he was trying to scrounge something.

Vdovushkin looked up from his work, cool and wide-eyed. He wore a white cap, to match his coat, and he had no number tags.

"But why did you wait till now? And why didn't you come yesterday evening? You know we can't take people in the morning. We've already sent the sick list to the PPS."

Shukhov knew all this. And he knew it wasn't any easier to get on the sick list in the evening either.

"But the trouble is, Nikolay, it doesn't feel so bad in the evening, when it ought to."

"What's wrong with you?"

"Well, when you get down to it, it's nothing in particular. I just feel rotten all over."

Shukhov was not one of those who's always hanging around the hospital block, and Vdovushkin knew it. But he was allowed to excuse only two men in the morning and he'd already excused them. And their names were on the list under the greenish glass on the table. There was a line drawn under them.

"You should have thought of this before. What do you think you're doing—coming here just before roll call? Here!"

Vdovushkin took one of the thermometers sticking through gauze in a jar, wiped the solution off it, and gave it to Shukhov.

Shukhov sat down on a bench by the wall, keeping on the very edge of it but just far enough in not to tip it over. He didn't choose this awkward place on purpose, but this was how he showed he was out of his depth in the hospital block and didn't expect very much.

Vdovushkin went on writing.

The hospital block was in the most out-of-the-way corner of the compound, and there was no noise from outside. There were no clocks ticking here—the prisoners weren't supposed to have any. The powers that be kept time for them. You didn't even hear a mouse scratching. They'd all been caught by the hospital cat appointed for the purpose.

Shukhov felt odd sitting by a bright lamp in such a clean room, where it was so quiet, and doing nothing for five whole minutes. He studied all the walls, but there was nothing. He looked at his jacket. The number on his chest had gotten a little worn. He'd have to have it redone if he didn't want trouble. He felt his beard. It had gotten pretty rough since that last visit to the bathhouse about ten days ago. But what the hell! There'd be another bath in about three days, and he'd have a shave then. Why waste time waiting in line at the barber's? He didn't have to look his best for anyone.

Then, looking at Vdovushkin's nice white cap, Shukhov remembered the field hospital on the river Lovat, how he'd gone there with an injured jaw and —dope that he was!—returned to his unit of his own free will. And he could have had five whole days in bed!

Now his one dream was to get sick for a couple of weeks, not fatally or anything that needed an operation, but just sick enough to be sent to the hospital. He'd lie there, he thought, for three weeks without moving, and even if the soup they gave you was a little thin it would still be great.

But then Shukhov remembered that there was no peace even in the hospital nowadays. There was a new doctor who'd come with a recent batch of prisoners—Stepan Grigoryevich, a loudmouth know-it-all who never stayed still himself and never let the patients alone either. He'd had the bright idea of putting all the walking cases to work around the hospital, making fences and paths and carrying earth to the flowerbeds. And in the winter there was always snow to clear. He kept saying that work was the best cure for illness.

What he didn't understand was that work has

23

killed many a horse. If he'd put in a little hard work laying bricks, he wouldn't go around shooting off his mouth so much.

Vdovushkin was still writing away. He really was doing something on the side, something that didn't mean much to Shukhov. He was copying out a long poem that he'd given the finishing touches to the day before and had promised to show Stepan Grigoryevich today—the man who believed in work as a cure-all.

This sort of thing could only happen in a camp. It was Stepan Grigoryevich who told Vdovushkin to say he was a medic and then gave him the job. So Vdovushkin started learning how to give injections to poor, ignorant prisoners who would never let it enter their simple, trusting minds that a medic might not be a medic at all. Nikolay had studied literature at the university and had been arrested in his second year. Stepan Grigoryevich wanted him to write the sort of thing here he couldn't write "outside."

The signal for roll call came faintly through the double windows. They were covered by ice. Shukhov sighed and stood up. He still felt feverish, but it looked as though he had no chance to get out of work. Vdovushkin reached for his thermometer and squinted at it.

"Look, it's hard to say—just under ninety-nine. If it were over a hundred, it'd be a clear case. But as things are I can't let you off. Take a chance and stay if you want. If the doctor takes a look at you and thinks you're sick, he'll let you off. But if not, it's the cooler for you. You'd be better off going to work."

Shukhov said nothing. He didn't even nod. He rammed on his cap and went out.

When you're cold, don't expect sympathy from someone who's warm.

The air outside hit Shukhov. The cold and the biting mist took hold of him and made him cough. It was 16 degrees below, while his own temperature was 99 above. He had to fight it out.

Shukhov trotted off to his barracks. The yard was absolutely empty. There wasn't a soul to be seen. It was that short, blissful moment when there was no way out any more, but people kidded themselves that there was and that there wouldn't be a roll call. The escort guards were sitting in their warm barracks, leaning their heads against their rifles—it was no picnic for them either to kick their heels on top of watchtowers in this freezing cold. The guards in the main guardhouse threw some more coal in the stove. The warders in the warders' room were finishing their last cigarette before going out to search the prisoners.

The prisoners—they were now dressed in all their rags, tied around with all their bits of string and their faces wrapped in rags from chin to eyes to protect them from the cold—were lying on their bunks on top of their blankets with their boots on, quite still and with their eyes closed. Just a few seconds more until the gang boss would yell: "Fall out!"

Nearly all the men in Barracks 9, including Gang 104, were dozing. Only the assistant gang boss, Pavlo, was busy, moving his lips as he counted something with the help of a small pencil. And on a top bunk the Baptist Alyoshka, Shukhov's neighbor, neat and cleanly washed, was reading his notebook in which he had half the Gospels copied down.

Shukhov raced in but didn't make a sound, and went to Pavlo's bunk.

Pavlo raised his head. "Didn't they put you in the cooler, Ivan Denisovich? And are you still alive?" (They simply couldn't teach Western Ukrainians to change their ways. Even in camp they were polite to people and addressed them by their full name.)

Pavlo handed him his bread ration from the table. There was a little white heap of sugar on top of it.

He was in a great hurry, but he answered just as politely (even an assistant gang boss is a big shot of sorts, and more depends on him than on the Commandant). He scooped up the sugar with his lips, licked the bread clean with his tongue, and put one leg on the ledge to climb up and make his bed. He looked at the ration, turning it, weighing it in his hand as he moved, to see if it was the full pound due him. Shukhov had had thousands of these rations in prisons and camps, and though he'd never had a chance to weigh a single one of them on a scale and he was always too shy to stick up for his rights, he and every other prisoner had known a long time that the people who cut up and issued your bread wouldn't last long if they gave you honest rations. Every ration was short. The only question was—by how much? So you checked every day to set your mind at rest, hoping you hadn't been too badly treated. ("Perhaps *my* ration is almost full weight today.")

"It's about half an ounce short," Shukhov figured, and he broke the bread in two. He stuck half inside his clothes—into his jacket, where he'd sewed in a little white pocket (the factory makes prison jackets without pockets). He thought of eating the other half, the one he hadn't eaten at breakfast, right away, but food eaten quickly isn't food. It does no good, doesn't fill you. He made a move to shove his half-ration in his locker, but changed his mind again. He remembered the orderlies had already been beaten up twice for thieving. The barracks was as public as the courtyard of an apartment building.

So, not letting go of the bread, Ivan Denisovich pulled his feet out of his felt boots, neatly leaving his foot-cloths and spoon inside them, climbed up barefooted, widened the little hole in his mattress, and hid the other half of his rations in the sawdust. He snatched his cap off his head, pulled a needle and thread out of it (this too was hidden carefully because they also checked prisoners' caps at inspection; once a warder had pricked himself on the needle and had been so angry he'd almost smashed Shukhov's head in). Three quick stitches and he'd sewed up the hole where the ration was hidden. Meanwhile the sugar in his mouth had melted. Shukhov's whole body was tense: at any moment the work-controller would start yelling in the doorway. Shukhov's fingers moved like lightning while his mind was running ahead thinking what he had to do next.

The Baptist was reading the Gospels not just to himself but almost aloud. Maybe this was for Shukhov's benefit (these Baptists love to spread a little propaganda):

"But let none of you suffer as a murderer, or as a thief, or as an evildoer, or as a busybody in other men's matters. Yet if any man suffer as a Christian, let him not be ashamed; but let him glorify God on this behalf."

One great thing about Alyoshka was he was so clever at hiding this book in a hole in the wall that it hadn't been found on any of the searches.

With the same swift movements, Shukhov hung his overcoat on a crossbeam, and from under the mattress he pulled out his mittens, a pair of thin foot-cloths, a bit of rope, and a piece of rag with two tapes. He evened the sawdust in his mattress a little (the stuff was heavy and hard-packed), tucked in his blanket all around, threw his pillow into place, then climbed down barefooted and started putting on his foot wrappings—first his good new foot-cloths and then on top the ones that weren't so good.

Then the gang boss cleared his throat loudly, got up and shouted:

"Snap out of it, 104! Out-si-ide!"

Right away everyone in the gang, whether snoozing or not, yawned and made for the door. The gang boss had been in camps for nineteen years, and he wouldn't chase you out to the roll call one second too early. When he said "Outside!" the time had really come.

As the men filed out without a word, clumping their feet, first into the corridor, then through the entryway and out to the steps—and after the boss of Gang 20 had also yelled "Out-si-ide!" the same way as Tyurin—Shukhov managed to put on his felt boots over his two pairs of foot-cloths. Then he put his overcoat over his jacket and tied it tightly with the rope (leather belts were taken away from prisoners—they weren't allowed in "Special" camps).

Shukhov finished all his chores and caught up with the last of the men in the entryway as they filed through the door and out to the steps. Bulky, wearing everything they had, they edged out in single file, and nobody was in a hurry to get out first. They trudged toward the yard and you could only hear the crunch of their boots.

It was still dark, though the sky in the east was getting bright and looked kind of green. A nasty little wind was blowing.

This was the toughest moment—when you lined up for roll call in the morning. Into the bitter cold in the darkness with an empty belly—for the whole day. You'd lost the use of your tongue. You didn't want to talk to anyone.

Near the perimeter a deputy work-controller was going frantic.

"Well, Tyurin, how long are we supposed to wait? Dragging your feet again, eh?"

Maybe Shukhov was frightened of him, but not Tyurin. He wouldn't waste his breath on him in this cold, and he just trudged on without a word. The gang came after him over the snow: tramp-tramp-tramp, crunch-crunch-crunch.

The boss must have slipped the fellow two pounds of fatback—you could see from the other gangs nearby that Gang 104 was being lined up in its usual place. It was only the other poor suckers who'd be marched off to the Socialist Community Development. God, it'd be hell there today, with a temperature of sixteen below and the wind and no cover at all!

The boss needed a lot of fatback to slip to the people in the PPS and still have enough left for his own belly. He didn't get any packages from home, but he was never short of fatback. It was always handed over to him right away by anyone in the gang who got some.

That was the only way you could live.

The chief work-controller made a note on a board.

"Tyurin, you have one sick today and twenty-three to go out. Right?"

"Twenty-three." The boss nodded.

Who was missing? Panteleyev wasn't there. But was he sick?

And right away there was a lot of whispering in the gang. Panteleyev the sonofabitch had managed to get out of it again. He wasn't sick at all—the security officer had kept him behind. He'd be squealing on somebody again.

They could easily send for him in the daytime—keep him there three hours if they liked—and nobody'd be any the wiser.

They worked it through the sick list.

The whole yard was black with prisoners' coats, and the gangs shuffled forward to be frisked. Shukhov remembered that he wanted to get the number on his jacket redone, and made his way over to the other side of the yard. There were a couple of men waiting in front of the artist. Shukhov joined them. These number tags were nothing but trouble. The

31

warders could spot you a long way off and the guards could write the number down when you did something wrong. And if you didn't have it redone, they'd put you in the cooler for not looking after it properly.

There were three of these artists in the camp. They painted pictures free for the higher-ups, and also took turns painting numbers at roll call. Today it was the old man with the little gray beard. When he painted the number on your cap, it was like a priest anointing your brow. He'd paint a little, and then a little more—and breathe on his fingertips. His knitted mittens were thin and his hands went stiff with cold so he couldn't make the numbers.

The artist gave Shukhov a new "S-854" on his jacket, and Shukhov, with his rope belt in his hand—not bothering to fasten up his coat because they weren't far from the friskers—went back to his gang. And he noticed at once that another fellow from his gang, Caesar, was smoking—not his pipe, but a cigarette—which meant there was a chance of cadging a smoke. But Shukhov didn't ask him outright. He stopped just next to Caesar, turned halfway toward him, and then looked past him.

He looked past as if he didn't care, but he could see how after every drag (Caesar was thinking about something and he wasn't taking many drags) the rim of red ash moved along the cigarette and burned it down nearer and nearer to the holder.

Right at this moment, that scavenger Fetyukov latched onto them, and stood right in front of Caesar and stared with burning eyes at his mouth.

Shukhov didn't have a shred of tobacco left and saw no chance of getting any today before the evening. He was tense all over from waiting, and right now he thought he'd rather have this butt than his freedom. But he wouldn't stoop as low as Fetyukov and look straight at the guy's mouth.

Caesar was a mixture of all races—whether he was a Greek, a Jew, or a gypsy you just couldn't tell. He was still young. He'd been a cameraman for the movies—but they put him inside before he'd finished shooting his first film. He had a big, black, bushy mustache. They hadn't shaved it off here because this was how he looked on the photo in his records.

"Caesar Markovich." Fetyukov drooled at him—he couldn't stand it any longer—"please give me one little drag!" He wanted it so badly his face was twitching all over.

Caesar's eyebrows went up a little—they were half-lowered over his black eyes—and he looked at Fetyukov. The reason he'd started smoking a pipe was so that people wouldn't bother him and cadge butts from him. It wasn't that he grudged them the tobacco, but he didn't like having his thoughts interrupted. He smoked to help his mind come up with great ideas. But all he needed to do was light a cigarette and right away he could see that look in people's eyes: "Leave a bit for me."

Caesar turned to Shukhov and said: "Here you are, Ivan Denisovich!"

He twisted the burning butt out of the short amber holder with his thumb.

Shukhov jumped (even though he'd thought Caesar would give it to him of his own accord). He took it with one hand, quickly and thankfully, and put his other hand underneath to guard against dropping it. He wasn't hurt because Caesar was squeamish about letting him smoke it in the holder (some people have clean mouths, others have foul mouths), and it didn't hurt his hardened fingers when the butt burned right down to them. The great thing was that he'd beaten that scavenger Fetyukov to it, and here he was now smoking away till it burned his lips. Mmmm. . . . The smoke seemed to go all through his hungry body and into his feet and his head.

Just as this wonderful feeling spread all through him, Ivan Denisovich heard a roar from the men:

"They're taking our undershirts away . . . !"

That's life in the camp. Shukhov had gotten used to it. Give 'em half a chance, if you didn't watch out they'd be at your throat.

Why shirts? They'd been issued by the Commandant himself . . . ! No, something was wrong. . . .

There were only two gangs ahead of them before the friskers, and everyone in Gang 104 spotted Lieu-

tenant Volkovoy, the disciplinary officer. He'd come
over from HQ and shouted something to the warders.
And the warders, who'd been taking it easy, now
really got busy and went for the men like wild ani-
mals. Their boss yelled:

"Open your shirts!"

They said even the Commandant was scared of
Volkovoy—let alone the prisoners and warders. Not
for nothing was he called Volkovoy.* And he always
looked at you like a wolf. He was dark and tall and
scowling, and always dashing around. He'd come at
you from behind the corner of the barracks, shouting: "What's going on here?" You couldn't keep out
of his way. In the early days he carried a whip of
braided leather as long as his arm. They said he beat
people with it. And he'd sneak up behind someone
during the evening roll call and let him have it in the
neck with his whip. "Get back into line, you scum."
Everybody would back away from him. The fellow
he'd whipped would take hold of his neck and wipe
off the blood and keep his trap shut so as not to get
shoved in the cooler on top of it.

Now, for some reason or other, he'd stopped going
around with the whip.

When it was freezing, the frisking routine was not
so tough in the morning—though it still was in the
evening.

The prisoners undid their coats and held them open. They marched up by fives, and five warders were waiting for them. They put their hands inside the prisoners' coats and felt their jackets. They patted the pocket (the only one allowed) on the right knee. They had gloves on, and if they felt something odd they didn't yank it out right away but asked, taking their time: "What do you have there?"

What did they hope to find on a prisoner in the morning? Knives? But knives don't get taken out of camp, they get brought in. What they had to watch out for in the mornings was people carrying a lot of food to escape with. There was a time when they were so worried about bread—a six-ounce ration for the noon meal—that an order was issued for each gang to make itself a wooden box and put everybody's bread together in it. It was anybody's guess why they thought this would help. Most likely the idea was to make things even tougher for people and add to their troubles—you took a bite out of it to put your mark on it, and threw it in the box. But all these hunks looked alike anyway. It was all the same bread. Then all the way you worried yourself sick about not getting your own piece back. And sometimes you got into a fight with people over it. Then one day three fellows escaped from the building site in a truck and took one of these boxes with them. So the bosses had all the boxes chopped up in the guardroom and then they went back to the old system.

In the mornings they also had to look out for anyone with civilian clothes under his camp uniform. They'd long ago taken away these clothes and they said you'd get them back when your sentence was up. But nobody'd ever been let out of this camp yet.

And another thing they checked for—letters you might try and slip to someone on the outside to mail. If they searched everybody for letters, they'd still be at it by noon.

But Volkovoy shouted to the warders to give them a real going over, and the warders quickly removed their gloves, told the men to open their jackets (where each man had taken a little of the warmth from his barracks) and undo their shirts. Then they began to feel around to see whether extra clothes had been put on against regulations. Each prisoner was allowed a shirt and vest, and anything extra had to come off—that was Volkovoy's order passed down through the ranks of the prisoners. The gangs that had gone ahead were lucky—some of them had already been checked out through the gates. But the rest had to open up. Anyone with extra clothing on had to strip it off right there in the freezing cold!

The warders got busy, but then they had trouble. The gates were clear now and the guards were yelling: "Come on, come on!" So 104 got a break from

Volkovoy. He told them to report if they had anything extra and hand it to the stores that evening with a note explaining how and why they'd hidden it.

Everything on Shukhov was regular issue. Let them look, he had nothing to hide. But they caught Caesar with a woolen shirt, and the Captain with some kind of jersey. The Captain kicked up a fuss, just like he used to on his ship—he'd only been here three months.

"You've no right to strip people in the cold! You don't know Article Nine of the Criminal Code!"

They had the right and they knew the article. You've still got a lot to learn, brother.

"You're not Soviet people," the Captain kept on at them. "You're not Communists!"

Volkovoy could take the stuff about the Criminal Code, but this made him mad. He looked black as a thundercloud and snapped at him:

"Ten days' solitary!"

And a bit quieter, he said to the chief warder: "You can see to that in the evening."

They didn't like putting people in solitary in the morning because it meant losing a day's work. So let him break his back all day and shove him in the cells at night.

The punishment block was nearby, on the left of the perimeter, a stone building with two wings. They'd finished building the second wing this autumn—one wasn't enough. The prison had eighteen blocks divided into small solitary cells. The rest of the camp was made of wood—only the prison was stone.

The cold had gotten under their shirts—there was no getting rid of it now. They'd just wasted their time wrapping themselves up. And Shukhov's back ached enough as it was. If only he could lie down in a hospital bed right now and sleep. That was all he wanted. With a nice heavy blanket.

The prisoners were standing in front of the gate buttoning and tying their coats, and the guards were waiting for them outside.

"Come on! Come on!"

And a work-controller was shoving them in the back.

"Come on! Come on!"

First there was one gate just at the perimeter. Then a second gate. And there were railings on both sides.

"Stop!" yelled one of the guards. "Just like a bunch of sheep! Line up by fives!"

Now it was getting light. On the other side of the guardhouse the escort's fire was almost out. They always lit a fire before roll call to keep warm and to get some light for the count.

A guard was counting in a loud, harsh voice: "One, two, three!"

The men peeled off by fives and filed through, so

whichever way you looked at them, from front or behind, you could see five heads, five backs, and ten legs.

A second guard, whose job it was to check the count, stood by the railings without speaking and just made sure the number was right.

The lieutenant stood still and watched. He'd come outside to doublecheck the count. That was the routine when they left the camp.

The men meant more to a guard than gold. If there was one man missing on the other side of the wire, he'd soon be taking his place.

The gang formed up again.

Now it was the sergeant who did the counting.

"One, two, three!"

Again groups of five men peeled off and marched in separate ranks.

The second-in-command of the escort checked them in on the other side.

Then there was another lieutenant. He was double-checking for the escort.

They couldn't afford to make a mistake. If they signed for one too many, they'd also had it.

There were escorts all over the place. They ringed the column going to the power station, shouldered their tommy guns and pointed them straight at your face. And then there were fellows with dogs. One of the dogs was baring his teeth like he was laughing at the prisoners. The escorts all wore short fur jackets. Only six of them had long sheepskin coats. They took turns wearing the long coats—they were for the ones who manned the watchtowers.

And once again they were lined up by fives and re-counted by the escorts.

"It's always coldest at dawn," the Captain explained. "Because that's the last stage of the loss of heat by radiation which takes place at night."

The Captain liked to explain things. He could figure out the phases of the moon, whether new or old, for any day of any year.

The Captain was clearly going downhill. His cheeks were caved in, but he kept his spirits up.

The cold here outside the camp, with a wind blowing, was biting Shukhov's face, even though it could take almost anything by now. He knew he'd have the wind in his face like this all the way to the power plant, so he put his piece of rag over it. Like many of the others, he had a rag with two long tapes to use when the wind was in his face. A rag like this really helped. Shukhov put it around his face, right up to his eyes, ran the tapes under his ears, and tied them behind his head. Then he covered the back of his neck with the flap of his cap and pulled up the collar of his jacket. Then he pulled down the front flap over his forehead. So all you could see was his eyes. He tightened his coat around his middle with the rope. Now everything was okay. Only his mittens were thin and his hands were already frozen. He rubbed them and clapped them together. He knew that at any moment he'd have to put them behind his back and keep them there for the rest of the way.

The commander of the escort read the daily "sermon," which everyone was fed up with:

"Your attention, prisoners! You will keep strict column order on the line of march! You will not straggle or bunch up. You will not change places from one rank of five to another. You will not talk or look around to either side, and you will keep your arms behind you! A step to right or left will be considered an attempt at escape, and the escort will open fire *without* warning! First rank, forward march!"

The first two escort guards must've already started along the road. In front the column swayed, men began to swing their shoulders, and the escort guards, twenty paces away at either side of the column and with ten paces between them, started off, their tommy guns at the ready.

There hadn't been any new snow for a week now, and the road was well trodden. They went around the edge of the camp and the wind hit them sideways. Hands behind backs and heads lowered, the column started off as if to a funeral. All you could see was the legs of the two or three people in front of you and the bit of trampled ground under your feet. From time to time a guard shouted: "Y-47!

Put your hands behind you!" "B-502! Keep up there!" Then even they began to shout less often. The wind whipped them and made it hard for them to see. And they weren't allowed to use face-rags. It was no fun for them either. . . .

Everyone talks in the column when it's warmer, no matter how much they're shouted at. But today everyone was bent forward, hiding behind the back of the man in front and thinking his own thoughts.

Even a prisoner's thoughts weren't free but kept coming back to the same thing, kept turning the same things over again. Will they find that bread in the mattress? Will the medics put me on the sick list this evening? Will they put the Captain in the cooler or not? And where did Caesar get that warm shirt? He must've gotten it out of someone in the stores with a bribe. Where else?

Since he'd had no bread at breakfast and what he'd eaten was cold, Shukhov felt really hungry today. And to keep his belly from whining and asking for food, he stopped thinking about the camp and thought instead about that letter he'd soon be sending home.

The column marched past the carpentry workshop built by the prisoners, past a block of living quarters (also built by the prisoners, but for "free" workers), and past the new club (also the work of prisoners, from the foundations to the decorations on the walls, but it was only the "free" ones who saw the movies there). The column came out into the steppe with the wind right in their faces, and there was a red sunrise. Bare white snow lay as far as the eye could see and there wasn't a tree in sight.

It was the beginning of a new year—1951—and Shukhov was allowed to write two letters home this year. He'd sent his last one off in July and had an answer in October. In Ust-Izhma there had been a different system—you could write once a month if you wanted. But what can you say in a letter? He hadn't written any more often there.

He'd left home on the twenty-third of June, 1941. One Sunday morning, people had come back from the church in Polomnya and said the war had started. They'd heard about it at the Polomnya post office, but in Temgenyovo—the village he lived in—no one had a radio before the war. Now, they wrote, there was "piped" radio in every hut, blaring all the time.

Writing now was like throwing stones into a bottomless pit. They fell down and disappeared, and no sound came back. What was the point of telling them what gang you worked in and what your boss was like? Now you had more in common with that Latvian Kilgas than with your own family.

Anyway, they only wrote twice a year, and you couldn't make out how they were getting along. They told you there was a new boss in the kolkhoz—but there was nothing new about that, they had a

44

new one every year. Or the kolkhoz had been "amal-
gamated"—but that was nothing new either, they
were always amalgamating them and splitting them
up again. Or somebody hadn't done his work quota
and had his private plot cut down to three-eighths
of an acre, and others had lost it all.

The thing Shukhov didn't get at all was what his
wife wrote about how not a single new member had
come to the kolkhoz since the war. All the youngsters
were getting out as best they could—to factories in
the towns or to the peat fields. Half the kolkhozniks
had not come back after the war, and those who had
wouldn't have anything to do with the kolkhoz—they
lived there but earned their money somewhere outside. The only men in the kolkhoz were the gang boss,
Zakhar Vasilyevich, and the carpenter, Tikhon, who
was eighty-four, had married not long ago, and even
had children already. The real work in the kolkhoz
was done by the same women who'd been there since
the start, in 1930.

The thing Shukhov just couldn't figure out was
these people living on the farm but working outside.
Shukhov had seen how it was on both individual and
collective farms, but the idea of peasants not working
in their own village—that he just couldn't take. Did
they go off to seasonal work or something? And what
did they do about getting the hay in?

His wife had told him they'd given up seasonal
work a long time ago. They didn't do any carpentry

any more—a thing their village was known for everywhere—and they didn't weave baskets any more. Who wanted that sort of thing nowadays? But now they were on to something new—painting carpets. Someone had got hold of some stencils in the war, and the thing had really caught on. More and more people were doing it and getting good at it. They didn't have any regular jobs and they helped in the kolkhoz for only a month in the year getting the hay in and harvesting. And they got a paper from the kolkhoz to say that for the other eleven months they'd been let off to take care of their own business and that they owed no taxes. They went all over the country and even flew in planes because their time was valuable. They raked in thousands of rubles painting carpets all over the place. They got 50 rubles for a carpet painted on some old sheet—these carpets, they said, could be finished in an hour. His wife hoped he'd be back one day and become one of these painters. Then they'd get out of the poverty with which she was struggling, send the children to technical school, and put up a new hut in place of the rotten old shack they were living in now. All these carpet painters were putting up new houses, and nowadays it cost you 25,000 rubles, not 5,000 like in the old days, to build a house near the railroad.

Then he wrote back to his wife and asked her to tell him how the hell he could be a carpet painter if he'd never been able to draw. And what was so great about these carpets? What did they put on them? His wife wrote back that any fool could make them. You just put on the stencil and dabbed paint through the holes. There were three kinds. One, the "Troika," had a picture of a carriage drawn by three horses with beautiful harness, and a hussar inside. The second was the "Stag," and the third was imitation Persian. There weren't any other patterns, but people all over the country were glad enough of even these and couldn't get their hands on them fast enough, because a real carpet doesn't cost 50 rubles—it costs thousands.

Shukhov would have given a lot to see these carpets.

In all the time he spent in camps and prisons, Ivan Denisovich had gotten out of the habit of worrying about the next day, or the next year, much less how to feed his family. The fellows at the top thought about everything for him, and it was kind of easier like that. Winter after winter, summer after summer —he still had a long time to go. But this business about the carpets upset him.

It looked like an easy, sure-fire way of making money. And it would be sort of wrong if he didn't keep up with the other fellows in the village. But deep down inside, Ivan Denisovich didn't want to have anything to do with this carpet business. You had to have a lot of gall and you had to know how to grease the right palm. Shukhov had been walking this earth for forty years. He'd lost half his teeth and he was getting bald. He'd never given or taken a bribe from anybody, and he hadn't learned that trick in the camp either.

Easy money doesn't weigh anything and it doesn't give you that good feeling you get when you really earn it. The old saying was true—what you don't pay for honestly, you don't get good value for. Shukhov's hands were still good for something. Back home he'd surely find himself work making stoves, or something in the carpentry line, or mending pots and pans.

The only catch was—if you'd been convicted with loss of civil rights, you couldn't get work anywhere and you weren't allowed back home. So maybe it would have to be those carpets after all.

The column had now arrived and stopped in front of the guardroom of the vast compound where the building site was. A little before that, two of the escorts in sheepskin coats had peeled off at a corner of the compound and made for the watchtowers at the far end. The prisoners would only be let in when the watchtowers had been manned. The officer in charge, with a tommy gun over his shoulder, went to the guardhouse. And there were great clouds of smoke pouring out of the guardroom chimney. They had a watchman there all night—a "free" worker, not a prisoner—so boards and cement wouldn't be stolen.

The big, red sun, sort of covered in mist, was slanting through the wires of the gate, across the whole compound and through the wire far over on the other side. Alyoshka, at Shukhov's side, looked at the sun and rejoiced. A smile came to his lips. His cheeks were sunken, he lived only on his ration and didn't earn anything extra. What was he so pleased about? On Sundays he spent all the time whispering with the other Baptists. The camp didn't worry them —it was like water off a duck's back.

Shukhov's face-rag had gotten all wet from his breath on the way, and it was frozen and had turned into an icy crust. He shoved it off his face onto his neck and stood with his back to the wind. He wasn't cold all through, but his hands were frozen in the thin mittens and the toes of his left foot had gotten numb—it was that left boot which had a hole burned in it and had to be sewed up again.

He had an aching pain all the way from the small of his back to his shoulders, so how could he work? He looked around and caught sight of the gang boss. He was at the end of the column. He had powerful shoulders and a large face. He looked grim. He didn't stand for any fucking nonsense in the gang, but he kept them pretty well fed and was always worried about getting them a good ration. He was doing his second sentence and he had lived practically all his life in the camps. What he didn't know about the camps wasn't worth knowing.

In a camp, your gang boss is everything. A good one can give you a new lease on life, but a bad one will finish you off. Shukhov had known Tyurin in the old Ust-Izhma days, only he wasn't in his gang there. And when prisoners sentenced under Article 58* had been switched from the ordinary camp at Ust-Izhma to the penal camp, Tyurin had picked him out. Shukhov never had any dealings with the Commandant, the PPS, the work-supervisors, and the engineers. The boss took care of all that sort of thing. He was like a rock. But he only had to raise an eyebrow or point a finger and you ran off to do what he wanted. You could cheat anyone you liked in the camp, but not Tyurin. That way you'd stay alive.

Shukhov wanted to ask him if they were going to work in the same place like yesterday or if they were going to another place, but he didn't dare break in on his thoughts. He'd only just wangled them out of the Socialist Community Development, and now he must have been figuring out how to get them good rates for the job. And their ration for the next five days depended on this.

Tyurin's face was covered with large pockmarks. He could face the wind without wincing—the skin on his face was tough like the bark of an oak tree.

The men in the column were slapping their hands together and stamping their feet. The wind was brutal. It looked like the guards were already up on all six watchtowers, but the men were still not being let inside. They must have another security drive on.

Here it was! The officer in charge of the escort came out of the guardroom with an inspector. They stood on each side of the gate and opened it.

"Line up by fi-i-ves! One! Two-o!"

The prisoners marched as though they were on parade—almost like soldiers. Once they got into the compound, they knew what to do without being told.

Just past the guardroom was the work office. The work-supervisor was standing there, calling over the gang bosses. And one of the foremen—a man called Der—went over to them. A real bastard. He was a prisoner himself, but he treated everybody else like dirt.

It was eight o'clock, maybe five minutes past (the steam engine they used to generate power had just given a blast on its whistle). The fellows in charge were scared stiff about the prisoners wasting time and ducking into shelters to keep warm. But the prisoners had a long day and took their time. As soon as they got into the compound they started bending down to pick up pieces of wood. It all came in handy for the stove back in camp.

Tyurin told his assistant, Pavlo, to come to the office with him. Caesar went along too. Caesar was rich, got two packages from home every month, and bribed all the right people. He had a soft job in the office, helping the fellow in charge of the work sheets.

The rest of Gang 104 took off like greased lightning.

The sun came up, red and hazy, over the empty compound. There were panels for prefabs covered over with snow, and the beginning of a brick wall they'd stopped work on. Then there was a broken part of a bulldozer. And a scoop and some metal scrap. There were ditches, trenches, and holes all over the place. The vehicle-repair shops were finished except for the roofs, and on a rise there was a power plant where they'd started on the second story.

Everybody was out of sight—all but the six sentries standing on the watchtowers and the men bustling around the office. This was the best moment in the day for a prisoner. They said the chief supervisor had threatened no end of times to pass out the work orders the evening before. But it never really worked, because they'd always change their minds by the morning.

But as it was they now had a moment to themselves. While they were figuring things out, you could find some warm spot and stay there for a spell before you started breaking your back. It was good if you could get near the stove to take your footcloths off, warm them a little, and then put them on again. Then your feet would be warm all day long. But even if you couldn't get to a stove it was still great.

Gang 104 went to the repair shops, where they'd put window panes in last autumn, and Gang 38 was making concrete blocks. Some of these blocks were lying around in their molds, others were standing upright, and there was steel meshwork for reinforcing the concrete. There was a high roof and an earthen floor, and it never really got warm here. But it was heated and they weren't stingy with the coal —not so people could get warm, but so the blocks would set better. There was even a thermometer, and on Sundays, if the prisoners weren't working, they had a "free" worker in there to keep the fire going.

Of course, the men of Gang 38 were hogging the stove, drying out their foot-cloths. Okay, so the rest of us have to sit in a corner. What the hell.

Shukhov perched on the edge of a wooden mold with his back to the wall. The seat of his padded pants had seen worse. When he leaned back, his coat and jacket pulled tight around his body, and on the left side of his chest, by his heart, he felt something hard. This was the hunk of bread in his inside pocket, the half of his morning ration he'd saved for the meal break. He always brought this much with him to work and never touched it before the meal break. He always ate the other half at breakfast, but today

53

he hadn't. He now saw it wasn't a saving at all. He felt a great hunger pang and wanted to eat it right away in this warm place. There were five hours till the meal break—it was a long time.

The pain in his back had now shifted to his legs and they felt all weak. If only he could get near the stove.

He put his mittens on his knees, undid his coat, untied the frozen face-rag from his neck, broke the ice to fold it up, and put it in his pocket. Then he took the bread in a piece of white cloth and cradled it behind the flap of his coat not to lose a single crumb, starting gradually nibbling at it and chewing it. He had carried the bread under two layers of clothes and warmed it with his own body, so it wasn't frozen at all.

In the camps he often remembered how they used to eat at home in the village—potatoes by the panful and pots of kasha, and in the early days before that, great hunks of meat. And they swilled enough milk to make their bellies burst. But he understood in the camps this was all wrong. You had to eat with all your thoughts on the food, like he was nibbling off these little bits now, and turn them over on your tongue, and roll them over in your mouth—and then it tasted so good, this soggy black bread. What had he eaten this eight years and more? Nothing at all. But the work he'd done on it!

He was busy with his six ounces of bread while his whole gang sat there on the same side of the shed.

Two Estonians, who were like blood brothers, were sitting on a low concrete block and smoking half a cigarette in turns from the same holder. They were both very fair, tall, and thin. Both had long noses and big eyes. They stuck together as though they couldn't breathe without each other. The gang boss never separated them. They shared all their food and slept on the top level of the same bunk. And in the column or at roll call or going to bed at night, they were always talking to each other in slow, quiet voices. But they weren't brothers at all, they'd only gotten to know each other here in the gang. One of them, they said, had been a fisherman, the other had been taken to Sweden by his parents when the Soviets came to Estonia and he was still a kid. But after he grew up he came back to Estonia of his own accord to get a college education.

Nowadays people say it doesn't matter where you come from and that there are bad people everywhere. But of all the Estonians he'd seen, Shukhov had never come across a bad one.

They were still sitting, either on the slabs or on the molds or just on the ground. You didn't feel like talking in the morning, and they were all wrapped up in their own thoughts. That scavenger Fetyukov had scrounged together quite a pile of cigarette butts from somewhere (he would even pick them up out of a spittoon without batting an eye), and now he was sorting them out on his knees and putting all the unburned tobacco in a piece of paper. Fetyukov had three children "outside," but they'd all disowned him when he was arrested, and his wife had married again. So there was no one to send him things.

The Captain kept looking at Fetyukov out of the corner of his eye, and then he yelled:

"Hey, what are you collecting all that crap for? You'll get syphilis. Throw it out!"

The Captain was used to giving orders and he always talked to people like this.

But Fetyukov didn't have to take orders from the Captain. He didn't get any packages either. So he just leered at him in a nasty way—he'd lost some of his teeth—and said, "Just wait, Captain, till you've been here eight years, you'll be doing the same thing. It's happened to better men than you."

Fetyukov was judging by himself, but maybe the Captain wouldn't go down so quickly.

"What's that? What's that?" Senka Klevshin said. He was rather deaf and couldn't hear what they were saying. He thought they were talking about the Captain's trouble at roll call. "You shouldn't have yelled at them like that." He shook his head sadly. "It would've blown over."

Senka Klevshin was a quiet fellow and he'd had a

very hard life. One of his eardrums had burst back in forty-one. Then he'd been taken prisoner, but he got away. They caught him and stuck him in Buchenwald. In Buchenwald he'd stayed alive by a miracle, and now he was here quietly doing his sentence. He said if you kicked up a fuss you were finished.

The only thing for you was to put your back into the work—that was for sure. If you tried to fight them, they'd break your neck.

Alyoshka dropped his face into his hands. He was praying.

Shukhov ate his ration nearly to the end, but he saved a bare crust, a round piece from the top, because you couldn't clean out the mush in your bowl with a spoon like you could with bread. He wrapped up the crust again in the white cloth for the next meal, stuck the cloth in the pocket on the inside of his jacket, buttoned himself up against the cold, and got ready. Let them send him to work now if they wanted. But he'd like it better if they waited a while.

Gang 38 got up. Some of them went to the cement-mixer, some to get water, some to the steel mesh-work.

But neither Tyurin nor Pavlo had come back to the gang. And though they had been sitting down for barely twenty minutes, and the workday—a short winter one—went on only till six, they all thought this had been wonderful luck, and the evening didn't seem far off now.

"You know there hasn't been a blizzard for a long time!" the Latvian Kilgas said with a sigh. He had red cheeks and was well fed. "Not one storm all winter! What kind of a winter is that?"

"Yes . . . not a single blizzard . . . not a single blizzard." A sigh went through the gang.

When there was a snowstorm in these parts, they didn't dare take you out of the barracks—let alone to work. Without a rope slung between your barracks and the mess hall, you could get lost. If a prisoner froze to death in the snow, the dogs could eat him for all anyone cared. But what if he escaped? It happened sometimes. When there was a storm, the snow was very, very fine, but in the snowdrifts it got packed down. Prisoners had gotten over the wire across these snowdrifts and made a run for it. But it's true they didn't get far.

Come to think about it, snowstorms weren't much use. They kept the prisoners locked in. The coal was late coming in and the warmth was blown out of the barracks. They brought no flour into the camp, and there was no bread, and things got fouled up in the mess hall. And it didn't matter how long the blizzard lasted—a couple of days or a week—they counted the days they lost as days off, and the men were marched out to work for the same number of Sundays in a row.

All the same, the men loved storms and prayed for them. Any time there was a low wind, everyone stared at the sky: "Give us some of the real stuff!"

Snow, they meant. The thing was that most of the time you only got a little powdered snow, not a real blizzard.

Now someone tried to horn in on Gang 38's stove, but they sent him packing.

Tyurin came in. He looked black. The men saw that they'd have to get down to work, and right away.

"Now then!" Tyurin looked around. "Are you all here, 104?" And not checking or counting—because nobody could have gone anywhere—he started giving them their working orders in a hurry. He sent the two Estonians and Klevshin and Gopchik to get the big cement-mixer from nearby and take it to the power plant. It was clear from this that the gang was being put on the unfinished power plant that they'd stopped work on in the autumn. He sent two others to the tool shop, where Pavlo was getting the tools. He told four others to clear the snow from around the plant, by the entrance to the generator room, and inside it, and from the ladders. He told another two to get the coal stove going there and to pinch some boards and chop them up. One man was to take cement there on a small sledge. Two were to carry water, two had to bring sand, and another had to clear the snow off the sand and break it up with a crowbar.

After all this, only two of them, Shukhov and Kilgas, the best workers in the gang, still hadn't gotten their orders. The boss called over and said: "Now, boys!" (He wasn't any older than them, but had this way of calling people "boys.") "After the meal break, you'll lay bricks on the second story, where Gang 6 left off the job last fall. But now I want you to cover up the windows in the generator room. There are three big windows there, and the first thing is to board them up with something. I'll send some others along to help, but start thinking what you're going to do it with. We'll use the generator room for mixing the mortar and warming up. If we don't manage to keep it warm, we'll freeze like stray dogs. Get it?"

He might have said something else, but Gopchik ran up to him—he was a kid of about sixteen with rosy cheeks—and complained that another gang wouldn't give them the cement-mixer and were fighting over it. So Tyurin went there.

Never mind how hard it was to begin the workday in such freezing cold, the thing was to get over the beginning—that was the important part.

Shukhov and Kilgas glanced at each other. They'd often worked together and they looked up to each other because they were both skilled men. Shukhov was a carpenter and Kilgas a bricklayer. It wasn't easy to find anything in the snow to board up those windows with. But Kilgas said:

"Ivan! I know a spot near those prefabs where

there's a big roll of roofing-felt. Hid it there myself. Let's go."

Kilgas was a Latvian but spoke Russian like a Russian. There was a village of Old Believers* near where he came from, and he learned it when he was small. He'd been in the camps only two years, but he knew his way around and he also knew that if you didn't help yourself, nobody else would. Kilgas and Shukhov had the same name and they called each other Ivan.

They decided to get the roofing-felt. But first Shukhov ran off to get his trowel from the half-finished repair shops. A trowel is a great help to a bricklayer when it's light and fits his hand. But on every working site it's a rule that at night you hand in all the tools they gave you in the morning. And it's a matter of luck what tool you get next day. But Shukhov had once managed to pull a fast one on the fellow in the tool shop and kept the best trowel for himself. Now he hid it in a different place every night and got it in the mornings if he was going to do any bricklaying. Of course, if they'd sent Gang 104 to the Socialist Community Development today, he wouldn't have been able to get it. But now he rolled away a small stone and stuck his fingers in a crack. There it was! He pulled it out.

Shukhov and Kilgas left the repair shops and went over to the prefabs. There was a cloud of steam from their breath. The sun had already come up, but there was a mist and they couldn't see the rays. They thought they saw something that looked like posts sticking out all around the sun.

"There are posts over there," Shukhov said, and jerked his head.

"We don't mind posts," said Kilgas, and he laughed. "As long as they don't stretch barbed wire over them, that's the thing to look out for."

Kilgas couldn't say a word without making a joke. The whole gang liked him for this. And the way all the Latvians in the camp looked up to him! But of course Kilgas ate pretty good with his two packages a month. He looked kind of healthy, just like he wasn't in a camp at all. It was easy for him to make jokes.

This site of theirs was really big. It took quite a while to get across it. On their way, they ran into some of the boys from Gang 82 who'd been put on digging up holes again. They didn't want very big holes—only a few feet deep. But the ground here was like stone even in summer, and now it was frozen stiff and it was impossible to dig. Hit it with a pick and it just skidded off. All you got was sparks, no earth at all. The fellows stood there by their holes and just looked around. There was nowhere to get warm and they couldn't leave. So they went at it again with their picks. That was the only way to keep warm.

Shukhov saw someone he knew among them—a fellow from Vyatka—and gave him a piece of advice. "Listen, fellows. Why don't you start a fire over these holes to thaw out the ground?"

"They won't let us." The man from Vyatka sighed. "They won't give us any wood."

"You should find some."

But Kilgas just spat: "Now tell me, Ivan, if our bosses had any sense, would they send people out to hack the ground with picks in cold weather like this?" He swore under his breath a couple of times and said nothing more. You couldn't talk much in this sort of cold. They went on till they came to the place where the prefab panels were buried under the snow.

Shukhov liked working with Kilgas. The only bad thing about him was that he didn't smoke and he never got any tobacco in his packages.

Kilgas really kept his eyes open. They picked up a board and then another, and there was the roll of roofing felt.

They took it out. But how could they carry it? It didn't matter about being seen from a watchtower. The guards only worried about people running away. That was their only concern. But inside you could chop up all the panels for firewood for all they cared. And if a camp warder ran into you, that didn't matter either. They were always on the lookout themselves for something that might come in handy. And the men couldn't care less either, nor could the gang bosses. The only people who worried were the chief work-supervisor, who wasn't a prisoner, and Der, the foreman, who was, and that beanpole Shkuropatenko. Shkuropatenko was no one in particular, just an ordinary prisoner, but he was paid for guarding the prefabs and stopping the prisoners from pinching them. It was this Shkuropatenko who was most likely to catch them.

"Look, Ivan, we can't carry it lengthways," Shukhov said. "Let's carry it upright with our arms around it and take it slow. We'll screen it with our bodies, and he won't see what we've got."

This was a good idea of Shukhov's. The roll was clumsy to carry, so they didn't pick it up but squeezed it between themselves like a third man and started off. All you could see from the side was two men walking close together.

"If the work-supervisor sees this on the windows later on, he'll guess what happened anyway," Shukhov said.

"What's that got to do with us?" Kilgas asked. "We can say it was already there when we came to the power plant. They're not going to tell us to pull it down."

That was true enough.

His fingers were numb in his mittens. He couldn't

feel them at all. And the cold had gotten into his left boot. Your boots were the main thing. His hands would warm up at work.

They walked over the untouched snow and came out on a sledge track that ran from the tool shop to the power plant. This meant they must have taken the cement there already.

The power plant was on a rise and it was right at the edge of the compound. No one had been in the power plant for a long time, and the snow all around it was unmarked. So the sledge track, the new path, and the deep footprints stood out more clearly and showed the men had gone that way. And they were already clearing snow with wooden shovels near the power plant and clearing a path for a truck.

It would be good if the hoist was working. But the motor had burned out and it looked like it hadn't been fixed. Which meant they'd once more have to carry everything up to the second story themselves— the mortar and the bricks.

The power plant had been there for two months, like a gray skeleton in the snow. But now Gang 104 had come. And what kept them going? Their empty bellies were held in by rope belts. The cold was fierce. There was no shelter and no fire. But they'd come and so life began again.

The cement-mixer was right there by the entrance to the generator room, but it had come apart. It was really rickety and Shukhov didn't think they'd get it there in one piece. The gang boss swore just for the hell of it, but he saw that nobody was to blame. Then Kilgas and Shukhov came up, carrying the roofing-felt between them. The gang boss was pleased and decided on a switch of jobs. He told Shukhov to fix the flue on the stove so they'd get it going as fast as possible. And Kilgas was told to patch up the mixer, with the two Estonians helping him. He gave Senka Klevshin an ax to cut laths to nail the felt on, because it wasn't the right width for the windows. Where could they get the wood? The work-supervisor sure wouldn't give them any just to make a shelter. The boss looked around and so did the others. All they could do was take the boards used as handrails for the ladders up to the second story. They'd just have to go up carefully if they didn't want to break their necks. There was no other way.

You might well ask why a prisoner worked so hard for ten years in a camp. Why didn't they say to hell with it and drag their feet all day long till the night, which was theirs?

But it wasn't so simple. That's why they'd dreamed up these gangs. It wasn't like gangs "outside," where every fellow got paid separately. In the camps they had these gangs to make the prisoners keep each other on their toes. So the fellows at the top didn't have to worry. It was like this—either you all got something extra or you all starved. ("You're not pulling your weight, you swine, and I've got to go hungry because of you. So work, you bastard!")

So when a really tough job came along, like now, you couldn't sit on your hands. Like it or not, you had to get a move on. Either they made the place warm within two hours or they'd all be fucking well dead.

Pavlo'd come with the tools already. All they had to do was pick out what they needed. And he also brought some pipes. True, there was nothing to fit 'em with, but there was a hammer and a small hatchet. They'd do it somehow.

Shukhov clapped his mittens together, placed the pipes end to end, and started fixing them up, dovetailing the joints. He'd hidden his trowel nearby. They were all friends in the gang, but that wouldn't stop one of them from working a switch. He wouldn't even put it past Kilgas.

The only thought in his head now—and his only worry—was how to fix the flues so they wouldn't smoke. He sent Gopchik to fasten the pipe at the window where it went out.

There was another potbellied stove in the corner with a brick flue. There was a red-hot iron plate on top of it to thaw out the sand and dry it. So they'd already got that one going, and the Captain and Fetyukov were carrying sand there in hods. You didn't need any brains to carry a hod. That was why Tyurin gave this work to people who used to run things before they got to the camp. Fetyukov was once some kind of a big shot in an office. He used to ride around in a car.

In the beginning Fetyukov tried to bully the Captain. But the Captain hit him in the teeth a couple of times, so they called it off.

The boys tried to get near the stove with the sand to warm up, but Tyurin stopped them. "Get on with the job first or I'll warm your asses for you!" he said.

Beat a dog once and you only have to show him the whip. The cold was vicious, but it had nothing on the gang boss. They all went back to work.

Shukhov heard Tyurin say in Pavlo's ear: "You stay here and keep 'em at it. I've got to go and fix the work rates."

More depends on the work rates than on the work itself. A clever boss who knows his business really sweats over these work rates. That's where the ration comes from. If a job hadn't been done, make it look like it had. If the rates were low on a job, try to hike 'em up. You had to have brains for this and a lot of pull with the fellows who kept the work sheets. And they didn't do it for nothing.

But come to think of it, who were these rates for? For the people who ran the camps. They made thousands on the deal and got bonuses on top for the officers. Like old Volkovoy, with that whip of his. And all you got out of it was six ounces of bread in the evening. Your life depended on them.

They brought two buckets of water, but it froze on the way over. Pavlo figured there was no point in carrying it. They could get it quicker by melting snow on the spot. They put the buckets on the stove.

Gopchik brought along some new aluminum wire, the kind electricians used.

He said: "Ivan Denisovich! This is good wire for spoons. Will you teach me how to make a spoon?"

Ivan Denisovich liked this little rascal Gopchik (his own son had died young, and he had two grownup daughters at home). Gopchik had been arrested for taking milk to Bendera partisans* in the woods. They gave him the same sentence a grownup got. He was friendly, like a little calf, and tried to please everybody. But he could be sly too. He ate the stuff in the packages he got, all by himself, at night. But come to think of it, why should he feed everybody?

They broke off some wire to make spoons and hid it in a corner. Shukhov made a sort of stepladder out of two planks and sent Gopchik to fix the chimney. Gopchik ran up the ladder like a squirrel. He banged in a nail, threw the wire over it, and fixed it around the pipe. Then Shukhov got busy and put

69

another piece of pipe on top where the flue came out. There was no wind today, but there might be tomorrow, and this was to stop the smoke from blowing back. This stove was for them, you see.

Senka Klevshin had already made some long laths. They told Gopchik to nail them on. He climbed up the windows, the little rascal, and shouted down.

The sun was higher now, the haze had gone, and there was no sign of those funny posts any more. And it was all crimson. They put the stolen wood in the stove and lit it. It was much more cheerful like that.

"It's only cows who get warm from the sun in January," Shukhov said.

Kilgas finished hammering the cement-mixer together, gave it a last tap, and shouted: "Listen, Pavlo, this job'll cost the boss a hundred rubles. I won't take less!"

Pavlo laughed. "You'll be lucky if you get a little extra on your ration."

"You'll get your bonus from the judge," Gopchik shouted down.

"Hold it, hold it," Shukhov yelled. (They were cutting the roofing-felt the wrong way.)

He showed them how to do it.

Some of the men were crowding around the other stove and Pavlo chased them away. He gave Kilgas some helpers, and told him to make hods for carrying the mortar up. He put two more men on to carry sand. He sent someone else up to clear the snow off the scaffold and the walls. And he got another man to shovel hot sand from the stove into the mixer.

They heard a motor outside. A truck with bricks was coming through. Pavlo ran out and waved his hands to show them where to unload.

They nailed on one strip of the felt and then another. But what protection do you get from roofing-felt? It's nothing but paper, really. All the same, it made a kind of solid wall. And it was darker inside, so the stove looked brighter.

Alyoshka brought some coal. Somebody shouted, "Pile it on!" Someone else yelled, "Don't, we'll get warmer from the wood!" He didn't know what to do, he just stood there.

Fetyukov squatted down by the stove, and put his felt boots right up to the fire, the dope. The Captain pulled him up by the scruff of the neck and pushed him over to the hods. "Go and carry sand, you bastard!"

To the Captain, camp work was like the navy. ("If you're told to do something, then get down to it!") He'd gotten pretty thin in the last month, but he was still doing his best.

Before long, all three windows were covered with felt. Now the only light came from the door. And the cold came in with it. Pavlo told them to cover the top part of the door and leave the bottom part open, just enough to get in and out with your head down. They did it.

Meantime three dump trucks had brought the bricks. Now the thing was how they could get them up to the top without a hoist.

"Hey, you bricklayers! Let's go up and take a look," Pavlo called.

Bricklaying was a job you could take pride in. Shukhov and Kilgas went up with Pavlo. The ladder was pretty narrow and Senka had taken away the handrails for firewood, so you had to stick close to the wall if you didn't want to fall off. And another thing was the snow had frozen to the rungs and made them slippery, so you couldn't get a grip with your feet. How the hell could they carry the mortar up?

They looked to see where to start laying. The fellows up there were shoveling away the snow already. They'd start over here. They'd have to hack the ice off the bricks and then scrape them clean.

They figured out how they'd get the bricks up. It'd be best if they didn't carry them up the ladder but had four fellows down below throw them to the first scaffold, then another two throw them up from there to the second story. And then there'd be two more fellows up here to carry them over to the walls. That'd be the quickest way.

There wasn't much of a wind up here, but you could still feel it. Enough to go right through you when you were working. But if you ducked down behind the wall it was a lot warmer.

Shukhov looked up to the sky and gasped. It was clear, and by the sun it was almost noon. It was a funny thing how time flew when you were working! He was always struck by how fast the days went in camp—you didn't have time to turn around. But the end of your sentence never seemed to be any closer.

They came down again and found everybody huddled around the stove, except the Captain and Fetyukov were carrying sand. Pavlo got mad and chased out eight of the fellows to get bricks, and told two of them to put dry cement and sand in the mixer. And he sent two others for water and coal.

Kilgas said to the fellows working with him: "Come on, let's finish these hods."

"Maybe I can give them a hand," Shukhov said to Pavlo.

"Okay." Pavlo nodded.

Then they brought in a can to melt snow for the mortar. They heard somebody say it was twelve o'clock already.

"It must be," Shukhov said. "The sun's right overhead."

"If it's right overhead," the Captain shot back, "that means it's one o'clock, not twelve."

"How come?" Shukhov asked. "Any old man can tell you the sun is highest at noon."

"That's what the old guys say!" the Captain snapped. "But since then, there's been a law passed and now the sun's highest at one."

"Who passed the law?"

"The Soviet Government!"

The Captain went out with the hods. But Shukhov wouldn't have gone on arguing anyway. Did the sun come under their laws too?

With a little more banging and hammering, they put together four hods.

"Okay, let's sit down and warm up," Pavlo said to the two bricklayers. "Senka, you'll be laying bricks after the meal break too. So sit down and get warm."

This time they had every right to sit down at the stove. They couldn't start the job before lunchtime anyhow, and if they started mixing the mortar too soon it'd freeze.

The coal in the stove was really going now and giving out a steady heat. But it only hit you near the stove—the rest of the shed was cold as ever.

All four of them took off their mittens and held their hands over the stove.

One thing you had to know was never to put your feet near the stove with your boots on. If they were regular boots, the leather cracked. And if they were felt, they got damp and steamed, and your feet didn't get any warmer. And if you put them right up to the fire, they got burned. Then you had to go along till

74

spring with a hole in them. There weren't any more where they came from.

"Why should Shukhov worry?" Kilgas was kidding him. "He's got one foot out of here already."

"Yeah, the one without the boot," someone butted in. They laughed. (Shukhov had taken off his left boot—the one with the hole in it—and was warming his foot-cloths.)

"Shukhov's sentence is almost up."

They'd given Kilgas twenty-five years. In the good old days it was always ten. But in 1949 they started slapping on twenty-five, regardless. Maybe you could last ten years and still come out of it alive, but how the hell could you get through twenty-five?

Shukhov sort of liked the way they pointed at him —the lucky guy nearly through with his sentence. But he didn't really believe it. Take the fellows who should've been let out in the war. They were all kept in till forty-six—"till further notice." And then those with three years who'd gotten five more slapped on. They twisted the law any way they wanted. You finished a ten year stretch and they gave you another one. Or if not, they still wouldn't let you go home.

But sometimes you got a kind of funny feeling inside. Maybe your number really would come up one day. God, just to think you might walk out and go home!

But old camp hands never said anything like that

out loud. Shukhov said to Kilgas: "Don't start counting up all the years you've got to go. Whether you'll be here for the whole twenty-five years or not is anybody's guess. All I know is I've done eight of mine, that's for sure."

So you just went on living like this, with your eyes on the ground, and you had no time to think about how you got in and when you'd get out.

In his record it said Shukhov was in for treason. And it's true he gave evidence against himself and said he'd surrendered to the enemy with the intention of betraying his country, and come back with instructions from the Germans. But just what he was supposed to do for the Germans neither Shukhov nor the interrogator could say. So they just left it at that and put down: "On instructions from the Germans."

The way Shukhov figured, it was very simple. If he didn't sign, he was as good as buried. But if he did, he'd still go on living a while. So he signed.

It happened like this. In February of forty-two his whole army was cut off on the Northwestern Front. They didn't send any food by air—there just weren't any planes. Then things got so bad they cut the hoofs off dead horses, soaked them in water to soften them up a little, and ate them. And they didn't have any ammo. The Germans tracked them down in the woods and rounded them up. Shukhov spent a couple of days in a POW cage in the forest. Then he got away with four others. They made their way through the forest and the bogs and got back to their own lines. And when they got there, a machine gunner opened fire. Two of them were killed on the spot and another died from his wounds. So only two of them made it. If they'd had any sense, they'd have said they got lost wandering in the woods—then nothing would have happened to them. But they told the truth and said they'd gotten away from the Germans. ("From the Germans, eh, you mother-fuckers!") If all five of them had made it, maybe they'd have checked their story and believed it. But just the two of them didn't have a chance. It was quite clear, they said, that they'd fixed up their escape with the Germans, the bastards.

Deaf as he was, Senka Klevshin could hear what they were talking about and said in a loud voice: "I got away three times and they caught me every time."

Senka had really been through the mill. Most of the time he didn't talk. He couldn't hear what people said and usually kept his mouth shut. So they didn't know much about him. All they knew was he'd been in Buchenwald and was in the camp underground there. He'd smuggled arms in for an uprising. Then the Germans hung him up with his arms tied behind his back and beat him.

"But what kind of camps were you in for those eight years, Ivan?" Kilgas asked. "Most of the time you've been in those ordinary camps with women, where they don't make you wear numbers. But eight years in a penal camp is a different story! Nobody's ever come out of this alive."

"We didn't have any women. All I ever saw was logs."

He stared into the fire and remembered his seven years in the North. The way he'd hauled logs for three years to make crates and railroad ties. The campfire used to flicker just like this in the lumber camp—when they had to work at night, that is. The Commandant's rule was—any gang that didn't do its quota in the daytime was kept on the job at night. They used to get back to camp after midnight and go out again in the morning.

"Don't kid yourself, fellows, it's easier here," he said in his funny way (he had that gap in his teeth). "Here you knock off the same time every day. Quota or no quota, they march you back to the camp. And the basic ration is six ounces more. You can live. So what if it is a 'Special' camp? Do the numbers bother you or something? They don't weigh anything."

"The hell it's easier!" Fetyukov hissed. (It was getting close to the meal break and they were all drawn up around the stove.) "They slit your throat here while you're in bed! You call that easy?"

"That happens only to squealers, not human be-

ings!" Pavlo put a finger up, like he was warning
Fetyukov.

It was true enough. This was a new thing in the
camp. Two stool pigeons had their throats slit right
in their bunks after reveille. And then they killed a
guy who was really straight. They must've gotten him
mixed up with somebody else. And one of the squealers beat it to the punishment block, and got them to
hide him there. It was a funny business, this. It never
happened in the ordinary camps. And it was something new here too.

The whistle on the steam engine went off. It didn't
go off full blast right away, but sounded kind of
hoarse at first, like it was clearing its throat.

They'd gotten through half a day. It was mealtime.

Hell, they'd been slow! They should've gone to
the mess hall long ago to get in line. There were
eleven gangs on the site, but the mess hall wouldn't
hold more than two at a time.

Tyurin hadn't come back yet. Pavlo gave a quick
look around and said: "Shukhov and Gopchik, you
come with me. Kilgas, when Gopchik gets back to
you, send the gang along at once!" Other fellows
moved into their places by the stove right away. It
could have been a woman the way they cuddled up
to it.

"Snap out of it!" somebody shouted. "Let's have
a smoke!"

They looked at each other to see who'd light up. But nobody did. Either they didn't have any tobacco or if they did they weren't letting anybody know.

Shukhov went out with Pavlo, and Gopchik trotted after them.

"It's a little warmer," Shukhov said when they got outside. "About one degree below, no more. Good weather for bricklaying."

They turned around and looked at the bricks. A lot had already been thrown up to the scaffold, and some were already on the floor of the second story.

Shukhov squinted up at the sun to check what the Captain had said about that law.

Out here in the open where there was nothing to stop it, the wind was blowing quite hard and bit your face, to let you know it was still January.

The mess hall on the working site was just a wooden shack with a stove in the middle. They'd nailed rusty metal sheets over it to cover the cracks. Inside it was split up into a kitchen and an eating room. There were no floors in either part. The earth had been trampled down by people's feet and was full of pits and bumps. And what they called the kitchen had just a square stove with a caldron.

The kitchen was run by two people—the cook and a sanitary inspector. When they left in the morning, the cook got an issue of groats from the big kitchen in the camp. It worked out to about two ounces a head—about two pounds for each gang. That is, a little over twenty pounds for everybody working on the site. The cook didn't carry that stuff himself on the two-mile march from the camp. He had a trusty who carried it for him. He thought it was better to slip an extra portion of the stuff to a trusty at the expense of the prisoners' bellies rather than break his own back. Then there was water and firewood to carry and the stove to light. The cook didn't do that either. He had other prisoners and "goners"* to do it. And they got their cut too. It's easy to give away things that don't belong to you.

The rule was you had to eat inside the mess hall. So they had to bring bowls from the camp every day. (They couldn't leave them on the site overnight because they'd be pinched by "free" workers.) So they brought about fifty of them over and washed them for each new batch that came in to eat. (And the man who carried the bowls got his cut.)

To stop people taking the bowls out of the mess hall, they put another trusty at the door. But they could watch as much as they liked, people took them out all the same. They talked their way past the trusty or slipped by while he wasn't looking. So on top of all this, they had another fellow who had to wander around the site and pick up dirty bowls and take them back to the kitchen. Both these got their cut too.

All the cook did was put groats and salt in the

caldron, and if there was any fat he split it between the caldron and himself. (The good fat never got as far as the prisoners. Only the bad stuff went in the caldron. So what did they care if the fat the stores handed out was no good!) Then his only job was to stir the mush when it was nearly ready. The sanitary inspector didn't even do that much. He just sat and watched. When the mush was ready, the cook gave him some right away and he could eat all he wanted. And so could the cook. Then one of the gang bosses—they took turns, a different one every day—came to taste it and see if it was good enough for the men to eat. He got a double portion too.

After all this, the whistle went off. Now the other gang bosses came and the cook handed them their bowls through a kind of hatch in the wall. The bowls had this watery mush in them. And you didn't ask how much of the ration they'd really put in it. You'd get hell if you opened your mouth.

The wind was whistling over the plain. It was hot and dry in summer and freezing cold in winter. Nothing would ever grow on that plain, even without the barbed wire. The only grain they knew about grew in the place where they handed out the bread ration, and oats ripened only in the camp stores. And you could kill yourself with work here or you could lay down and die, but you'd never beat any more food out of this earth than what the Commandant handed over. And you didn't get that in full either, what with the cooks and all their pals. They stole all the way down the line—out here on the site, in the camp, and in the stores too. And you never saw these thieves doing any hard work. But it was you who sweated, and you took what they gave you and didn't hang around the hatch.

It was every man for himself.

Pavlo, Shukhov, and Gopchik went into the mess hall. The men were standing jammed up against each other—so many backs you couldn't even see the low tables or the benches. Some were eating sitting down, and others on their feet. Gang 82, who'd been digging holes in the open the whole morning, came in first after the whistle and grabbed all the seats. Even if they'd finished eating, they still hung around. Where else could they get a little warmth? The others were swearing at them. But you might just as well swear at a brick wall. What did they care? It was better here than out in the cold.

Pavlo and Shukhov pushed their way through. They'd come at a good time. One gang was getting its stuff, another was waiting in line, and the assistant gang bosses were standing by the hatch too. This meant 104 was next in line.

"Bowls! Bowls!" the cook shouted through the hatch, and people were shoving them at him from the other side. Shukhov got some bowls too and shoved them through the hatch, not to get anything extra for himself but to speed things up. Some of the cook's pals were washing bowls in the kitchen. And they weren't doing it for nothing.

The assistant gang boss in front of Pavlo was getting the stuff for his men, and Pavlo shouted back over people's heads: "Gopchik!"

"I'm here," Gopchik answered from the door. He had a squeaky little voice like a young goat.

"Call the gang!"

Gopchik ran off.

The mush they were giving out today wasn't bad. It was the best kind, made of oats. It didn't come very often. It was usually *magara* twice a day, or flour mixed with water. These oats were more filling, and that's what counted.

The amount of oats Shukhov fed to horses when he was a boy, and he never thought he'd long for a handful himself one day!

"Bowls! Bowls!" they were shouting from the hatch.

Gang 104's turn was coming. The assistant gang boss in front took his special double portion and cleared out.

This came out of their bellies too. And again nobody said a thing. Every gang boss had the right to a double portion, and he could eat it himself or give it to his assistant. Tyurin gave his to Pavlo.

Now Shukhov squeezed through to one of the tables, chased away a couple of "goners," asked another prisoner to have a heart and go away, and cleared enough room at the table for twenty bowls. (First he'd put twelve close together, then another six on top of them, and another two on top of those.) Next he had to take the bowls from Pavlo, count them over and make sure nobody swiped one from the table. Or knocked one off with his elbow. And on both sides men were getting up from the bench or sitting down to eat. He had to keep an eye on them to be sure they were eating their own stuff and not what belonged to his gang.

"Two! Four! Six!" the cook counted on the other side of the hatch. He gave out two at a time. It was easier not to lose count that way.

"Two, four, six," Pavlo said after him into the hatch. And he passed them over to Shukhov two by two, and Shukhov put them on the table. Shukhov didn't count out loud, but he kept a closer check than anybody.

"Eight, ten."

Why wasn't Gopchik there with the gang yet?

"Twelve, fourteen."

Then they ran out of bowls in the kitchen. Over Pavlo's head and shoulders, Shukhov could see the cook put two bowls down on the ledge and stop with his hands still on them, like he was thinking about something. He must have turned around to bawl out the dishwashers. Just then a pile of empty bowls was shoved at him through the hatch. He let go of the two bowls and passed the empty ones back.

Shukhov took his eyes off the pile of bowls he had on the table, turned around and threw one leg over the bench, grabbed both the bowls and said, "Fourteen," but not loud. This was meant for Pavlo and not for the cook.

"Hey! Where're you going with those?" the cook yelled.

"They're ours! They're ours!" Pavlo shouted back.

"They may be yours, but don't make me lose count!"

"Well, it was fourteen," Pavlo said, and shrugged his shoulder. He wouldn't have gone in for this kind of thing on his own because he had his position to think of. But he went along with Shukhov, and he could always get out of it by saying it wasn't his fault.

"I already said fourteen," the cook yelled like crazy.

"Sure you did, but you didn't give them out, you had your hands on them!" Shukhov shouted. "Come over here and count 'em if you don't believe me. They're all over here on the table!"

While he was shouting like this at the cook, Shukhov saw the two Estonians coming through the crowd and he slipped the two extra bowls to them. Then he turned back to the table again and counted up to see if all the bowls were still there. But his neighbors had been slow, they hadn't pinched anything, though they easily could have.

The cook stuck his ugly red puss through the hatch.

"Where are they?" He was getting nasty.

"Take a look. You're welcome!" Shukhov shouted. "Get out of the way! Don't block his view!" He gave somebody a shove. "Here's two!" He held up the two bowls from the top. "And here's the other twelve by rows of four. Count em!"

"Where's your gang?" The cook took a sharp look at him through the little space in the hatch. The reason it was narrow was to stop anybody from looking in to see how much was left in the caldron.

"They're not here yet," Pavlo said and shook his head.

"What the fucking hell do you mean taking bowls before your gang comes?" He was mad.

"Here they are now," Shukhov shouted.

They could all hear the Captain yelling in the doorway like he was still on the bridge of his ship: "What's everybody hanging around for? You've had your meal, so get out! Give somebody else a chance!"

The cook grumbled something, straightened up, and now all you could see was his hands in the hatch again.

"Sixteen, eighteen."

Then he ladled out the last one, a double helping. "Twenty-three. That's it! Next!"

The other fellows in the gang pushed through and

Pavlo handed their bowls to them. Some went over to another table, and he had to pass the bowls over people's heads.

In summer they sat five men to a bench. But now, in winter, their clothes were so bulky they barely managed four. Even so, they didn't have much elbow room for their spoons.

Figuring he had a claim on one of the bowls he'd finagled, Shukhov started eating his own portion fast. He lifted his right leg, pulled the spoon marked "Ust-Izhma, 1944" from the top of his boot, took off his cap, tucked it under his left arm, and stirred his mush.

Now he had to give all his time to eating. He had to scrape the stuff out from the bottom, put it carefully in his mouth, and roll it around with his tongue. But he must hurry so Pavlo would see he'd finished and give him a second bowl. And now Fetyukov, who'd come in with the Estonians and seen the business with the two extra bowls, stood right across from Pavlo and ate standing up. He kept looking over at them. He was trying to make Pavlo see he ought to get at least half a helping more, if not a full one.

But Pavlo—he was a young, dark fellow—just went on eating, and you couldn't tell from his face if he could see the people next to him or not, and if he remembered about the two extra bowls.

Shukhov finished the first bowl. Maybe it was because he'd set his mind on two helpings, but this first one just didn't fill him the way oatmeal always did. He reached into his inside pocket, took the round piece of crust out of the white cloth, and started mopping up all the bits of oatmeal still sticking to the bottom and sides of the bowl. When he'd gotten enough of it together, he licked it all off and then started over again. When he was through, the bowl was clean like it had been washed, except it wasn't so shiny. He handed the bowl over his shoulder to one of the dishwashers and went on sitting there for a minute with his cap still off.

Though it was Shukhov who'd finagled the bowls, it was Pavlo who doled them out.

Pavlo kept him dangling a little longer, till he'd finished eating. Pavlo didn't lick his bowl, only the spoon. Then he put it away and crossed himself. Then he touched the two extra bowls—there were so many others on the table, he couldn't shove them across—sort of telling Shukhov they were his.

"Ivan Denisovich, take one for yourself. And take the other over to Caesar."

Shukhov remembered they had to take one bowl to Caesar in the office. (Caesar thought it was beneath him to go to the mess hall, either here or in the camp.) He hadn't forgotten that, but when Pavlo touched the two bowls his heart missed a beat. Maybe Pavlo was going to let him have both. But now he came down to earth again.

So he bent down over this windfall that was now

his by right and took his time over it, and he didn't even feel it when fellows from the new gang coming in pushed him. The only thing that worried him was that Fetyukov might get an extra helping. You couldn't beat Fetyukov when it came to scrounging, though he didn't have the guts to pinch anything.

The Captain was sitting near them. He'd finished his mush some time ago and didn't know the gang had gotten any extras. And he didn't keep looking around to see what Pavlo still had there. He was feeling nice and warm here and didn't have the strength to get up and go out again in the freezing cold or back to that power plant where there was no warmth at all. And now he was taking up space somebody else could use from the new gang coming in—just like the people he'd tried to chase out only five minutes ago when he shouted at them. He hadn't been in the camp very long. It was moments like this (though he didn't know it) that were very important for him. This was the sort of thing that was changing him from a bossy, loudmouth naval officer into a slow-moving and cagey prisoner. He'd have to be like this if he wanted to get through his twenty-five years in camp.

People were already shouting at him and shoving him in the back to get him to leave his place.

Pavlo said: "Captain! Hey, Captain!"

The Captain started, like out of his sleep, and

turned around. Pavlo handed him the mush without asking if he wanted it or not.

The Captain's eyebrows went up, and he looked at the stuff as if he'd never seen anything like it in all his life.

"Take it, take it," Pavlo said to set his mind at rest. He grabbed the last bowl of mush for the gang boss and went out.

The Captain had a kind of shamefaced smile on his chapped lips. (He'd sailed ships all around Europe and the Arctic.) He bent down over the half bowl of thin oatmeal mush and he was happy. There was no fat in it—just water and oats.

Fetyukov gave Shukhov and the Captain a nasty look and went off.

But to Shukhov's way of thinking, it was only right to give it to the Captain. The time would come when he'd learn the ropes, but as it was he didn't know his way around yet.

Shukhov had a faint hope that Caesar might give the Captain his mush too. But then why should he, seeing he hadn't had a package for two weeks now?

After he finished his second helping he cleaned the bottom and sides of the bowl with his crust of bread, licking it all the time. Then he ate the crust as well. After he was all through, he took Caesar's cold mush and went off.

"Going to the office," he said to the trusty at the

door, who wasn't supposed to let people through with bowls, and pushed past him.

The office was a wooden shack next to the guard-room. Smoke was still belching out of the chimney, just like in the morning. The stove was kept going by an orderly who also worked as a messenger and was given a piece rate for this. The office never ran out of firewood.

The outside door and then the inside door (it was padded with rope) creaked when Shukhov opened them. He slipped in and brought a billowing cloud of steam with him, and pulled the door to fast (so they wouldn't yell at him "Shut the door, you bastard!").

It was real hot inside—like a steam bath, he thought. The sun looked playful through the melting ice on the windowpanes—it wasn't angry like on top of the power plant. And smoke from Caesar's pipe was curling through the sunbeams like incense in a church. The stove was glowing red-hot—they'd stoked it up so much, the bastards. And the flues were red-hot too.

Just sit down for a minute in that heat and you'd go to sleep right away.

There were two rooms in the office. The second one, the work-supervisor's, had the door slightly ajar. You could hear him shouting in there:

"We're overspending on wages and we're over-spending on building materials. The prisoners are chopping up expensive boards and prefab walls and burning them in their shelters. But *you* don't see a thing. And the other day they were unloading cement at the depot in a high wind and carting it a few yards in hods. So we were ankle-deep in cement all over the area around the depot, and they went away covered in the stuff. All this waste!"

From the sound of things the supervisor was having a conference. Must have been with the foremen.

An orderly was snoozing on a bench in a corner by the door. Next to him was B-219, Shkuropatenko. He was like a bent beanpole. He was staring through the window and watching so nobody pinched his precious prefabs. He'd been caught napping over the roofing-felt, the sucker!

There were two bookkeepers—they were prisoners too—toasting bread on the stove. They'd rigged up a wire frame so it wouldn't burn.

Caesar was lolling in his chair at a table and smoking his pipe. He had his back to Shukhov and couldn't see him.

K-123 was sitting across from him. He was a scrawny old man who'd done twenty years. He was eating mush.

"You're wrong, pal," Caesar was saying, and he was trying not to be too hard on him. "One must say in all objectivity that Eisenstein is a genius. Now isn't *Ivan the Terrible* a work of genius? The *oprichniki** dancing in masks! The scene in the cathedral!"

"All show-off!" K-123 snapped. He was holding

his spoon in front of his mouth. "Too much art is no art at all. Like candy instead of bread! And the politics of it is utterly vile—vindication of a one-man tyranny. An insult to the memory of three generations of Russian intellectuals!" (He ate his mush, but there was no taste in his mouth. It was wasted on him.)

"But what other treatment of the subject would have been let through . . . ?"

"Ha! *Let through,* you say? Then don't call him a genius! Call him a toady, say he carried out orders like a dog. A genius doesn't adapt his treatment to the taste of tyrants!"

"Hm, hm!" Shukhov cleared his throat. He was afraid to butt in on this learned conversation. But he couldn't just go on standing there.

Caesar looked around and stretched out his hand for the mush, as if it had just come to him out of thin air. He didn't even look at Shukhov and went back to his talk.

"But listen! It's not *what* but *how* that matters in art."

K-123 jumped up and banged his fist on the table.

"No! Your *how* can go to hell if it doesn't raise the right feelings in me!"

After he'd handed over the mush, Shukhov went on standing there for just as long as was decent. He thought Caesar might give him a little tobacco. But

Caesar'd clean forgot he was standing there behind him.

So Shukhov turned and walked out quietly.

It wasn't bad outside. Not too cold. They'd do all right with the bricklaying today.

Shukhov walked along a path. He saw a chunk of metal in the snow. It had broken off a steel plate. He could think of no particular use for it, but you never know when something might come in handy. He picked it up and put it in the knee pocket of his pants. He'd hide it in the power plant. It's better to be thrifty than wealthy.

When he got to the power plant, he first took his trowel from its hiding place and stuck it behind his rope belt. Then he ducked into the shed where they made the mortar.

It seemed dark here, coming out of the sun, and no warmer than outside. And it felt damper somehow.

The men were huddled around two stoves the one Shukhov had set up here and the other one where the sand, steaming a little, was being heated. Those who didn't have a place were sitting on the edge of the trough where the mortar was mixed. The gang boss was sitting right by the stove eating his mush. Pavlo'd warmed it up for him.

The men were whispering among themselves.

They were a little more cheerful. They told Ivan Denisovich that the boss had managed to wangle better rates for them. He'd come back from the office in a good mood.

What sort of work he'd dreamed up for them was his business. What had they done in the morning? Nothing. They had nothing coming to them for the stove and the shelter. This was for them and didn't count as output. But something had to go down on the work sheet. Maybe Caesar would monkey with the cards for them too. The boss was respectful to him and there must be a reason for it.

Tyurin got "better rates," which meant they'd have good bread rations for five days. Well, maybe four. The higher-ups always cheat on one day out of five. On the "guaranteed" day off they put everybody on an equal footing, both good and bad. Just-so-nobody-gets-upset sort of thing, and share and share alike. They saved something on this and it came out of the men's bellies. So what? A prisoner's belly can stand anything. Get by somehow today and eat tomorrow. That's what they all dream when they lie down to sleep on the day off.

But come to think of it, they ate four days for every five they worked.

The gang was quiet. The guys with tobacco were smoking on the sly. They were huddling in the darkness and looking at the fire. Like one big family. It was a family, your gang. They were listening to the boss tell a story to a couple of the guys near the stove. He never wasted his breath on talk, and if he got going with a story it meant he was in a good mood.

And he'd never learned to eat with his cap on, the boss. He looked old without it. His head was shaved, like everybody else's, and by the light of the stove you could see the stubble was all gray.

"I was scared enough in front of the Major," he was saying, "but now I was up in front of the Colonel. 'Private of the Red Army Tyurin reporting,' I say. He stared at me and his eyebrows were fierce. 'What's your first name and your father's first name?' he asks. So I tell him. 'And your date of birth?' I tell him that too. I was twenty-two then, in 1930, just a kid. 'Well, how are you serving,* Tyurin?' 'I serve the working people!' He blew up and banged both his fists on the table: 'You serve the working people, but what are you, you bastard?' I boiled up inside, but I held myself in: 'Machine-gunner first class. Top marks in military and political . . ,' I say. 'What do you mean, first class, you swine? Your father's a kulak! Here are the papers from Kamen! Your father's a kulak and you ran away. They've been hunting you for two years now!' I got pale all over and said nothing. I didn't write home for a year so they wouldn't get on my track. I didn't know whether my folks were still alive and they knew nothing about me. 'You've got no conscience,' he bawls, 'deceiving the Workers' and Peasants' Government!' and his four shoulder straps were shaking. I thought he was going to beat me up. But he didn't. He signed an order for me to be kicked out in six hours. . . . It was November. They stripped off my winter uniform and gave me a worn-out summer one with an overcoat that was too short. I was all fucked up and didn't know I could have kept the other uniform and told them to go to hell. . . . And they gave me a lousy discharge: 'Dismissed from the ranks as the son of a kulak.' Some chance of getting a job with that! It was a four days' train ride home and they didn't give me a ticket. They didn't give me any food either. They just gave me my last meal in the barracks and kicked me out.

"By the way, in thirty-eight I met my old sergeant in the Kotlas transit camp. He'd gotten ten years too. Well, I got to know from him that this Colonel and his commissar were both shot in thirty-seven. It didn't make much difference then whether they were proletarians or kulaks, whether they had a conscience or not. . . . I crossed myself and said: 'There's a God in heaven after all. He's long-suffering, but when he hits you, it hurts.' "

After the two bowls of mush, Shukhov wanted a

smoke real bad. And figuring he could buy a couple of mugs of tobacco from the Latvian in Barracks 7 and pay back the loan later, he said quietly to the Estonian fisherman:

"Listen, Eino, lend me a little till tomorrow—just enough for one cigarette. You know I won't gyp you."

Eino looked Shukhov straight in the eyes and then looked at his bosom pal. They always shared and shared alike and wouldn't use a single shred of tobacco without the other knowing. They said something to each other under their breath and Eino got out his pouch stitched with pink cord. He took some tobacco and put it in Shukhov's hand. Then he had another look and threw in a few more strands —just enough to make a cigarette but no more.

Shukhov had some newspaper. He tore a piece off, rolled a cigarette, and lit it with a cinder that had fallen between the boss's feet. And then he dragged and dragged on it, over and over again! He had a giddy feeling all over his body, like it was going to his feet as well as his head.

The minute he started to smoke, he saw a pair of green eyes flashing at him from the other end of the shed. It was Fetyukov. He might have taken pity on that scavenger, but he'd been cadging already today. Shukhov had seen him at it. Better leave the butt for Senka Klevshin. He couldn't hear the boss's story, poor devil, and was just sitting there in front of the stove with his head on one side.

The boss's face—it was all pockmarked—was lit up by the fire. He told his story without pity, like it wasn't about himself:

"I sold the junk I had for a quarter of its worth to a dealer and bought two loaves of bread on the black market. They'd brought in ration cards by then. I thought I'd get home by riding freights, but they'd just put out some tough laws against that. And you couldn't get tickets then, remember, even with money, never mind without it. They only gave 'em out for vouchers or for travel orders. You couldn't even get into the station—they had militiamen at the gates and guards on both sides of the tracks. The sun was going down and the puddles were freezing over. Where could I spend the night? I climbed a brick wall, jumped over with my two loaves of bread, and got into the station latrine. I hid out there for a while, but there was no one after me. Then I came out, just like I was a passenger, a soldier in uniform. The Vladivostok-Moscow was standing right there on the track. There was a great scramble for getting boiling water and people were hitting each other on the head with their kettles. There was a girl in a blue dress with a large teakettle, but she was too scared to try and get some water—afraid she'd get her tiny little feet scalded or crushed. 'Here, hold these,' I said and gave her my loaves. 'I'll get it for you!' By the time I got it, the train was just ready to go. She was standing there with my loaves and crying and didn't know what to do with them—she wouldn't have minded losing her kettle. 'Run!' I shouted, 'Run! I'll come after you!' So she made a dash for the train. I caught up with her and pushed her into the coach—the train was already moving—with one arm and then jumped on myself. The conductor didn't try to hit me over the knuckles or push me off—there were other soldiers in the coach and he thought I belonged with them."

Shukhov nudged Senka in the ribs for him to take the butt, poor devil. He gave it to him in his wooden holder. Let him have a draw on it, it didn't matter. Senka was a real character. He put his hand on his heart and bowed like an actor on a stage.

The boss went on: "There were six other girls in the compartment—it was reserved—students from Leningrad they were, going back home from some fieldwork or other. They had bread and butter and all kinds of fancy things on the tables in front of them. Their coats were hung up on hooks and they had covers on their suitcases. They didn't know what real life was—they'd had it easy all the way. . . .

We talked and joked and had tea together. Then they asked me what coach I'd come from. I sighed and told them the truth. 'Girls,' I said, 'in the coach I come from you can't live. . . .' "

It was quiet in the shed. The stove was blazing.

"After a lot of oh-ing and ah-ing they had a little talk and hid me under their coats on the top bunk. They got me all the way to Novosibirsk like that. . . . By the way, I met one of those girls later in one of the Pechora camps and did her a favor in return. She'd been picked up in thirty-five over the Kirov business* and she was just about on her last leg doing 'hard.' I managed to fix her up in one of the workshops."

"Maybe I should start making the mortar?" Pavlo asked the boss in a whisper.

But the boss didn't hear him. He went on with his story:

"I got home late one night and went in through the back garden. I went away again the same night and took my kid brother with me. I took him down south, to Frunze, where it's warmer. I had no food for him or me. They were making tar in a caldron on one of the streets there, and a gang of young thugs was sitting around it. I went and sat down with them and I said, 'Listen here, gentlemen of the gutter, take this kid brother of mine and give him an education. Teach him how to live.' And they did. Sorry I didn't go off with them myself. . . ."

"And you never saw your brother again?" asked the Captain.

The boss yawned.

"No, I never saw him again." And he yawned once more. Then he said: "Don't worry, boys! We'll make ourselves at home in the power plant. You boys making the mortar'd better get busy. Don't wait for the whistle."

That's how it was in your gang. The higher-ups had a job to get a prisoner to work even in working hours, but your boss only had to say the word, even if it was the meal break, and you worked. Because it was the boss who fed you. And he wouldn't make you work if you didn't have to.

If they didn't start making the mortar before the whistle, the men laying the bricks would be held up.

Shukhov sighed and got up.

"I'll go and clear the ice."

He took a hatchet and a wire brush for the ice, a bricklayer's gavel, a yardstick, and a plumb line.

Kilgas looked at Shukhov and made a face as if to ask what he meant by going on ahead of the boss. Kilgas didn't have to worry about food for the gang. What did *he* care how much bread they got? He did all right on packages from home.

All the same he got to his feet. He knew he couldn't hold up the gang just for himself.

"Hold it, Ivan, I'll come along too," he said.

Trust old moonface. If he'd been working for himself, he'd have been on his feet even sooner. (And another reason Shukhov was in a hurry—he wanted to grab the plumb line before Kilgas. They'd only gotten one from the tool shop.)

"Will there be three laying the bricks?" Pavlo asked the boss. "Should we put another man on? Or won't there be enough mortar?"

The boss frowned and thought a while. "I'll be the fourth man myself, Pavlo. And what's that about the mortar? The mixer's so big you could put six men on the job. You take the stuff out at one end while it's being mixed at the other. You just see we're not held up a single minute!"

Pavlo jumped up. He was a young fellow and he had a good color. He still hadn't been too hard hit by life in the camps. And his cheeks were still round from eating those Ukrainian dumplings back home. "If you lay bricks," he said, "I'll make the mortar. And we'll see who works the fastest! Where's the biggest shovel around here?"

That's what these gangs did to a man. There was Pavlo who used to carry a gun in the forests and make raids on villages. Why the hell should he kill himself with work in this place? But there's nothing you wouldn't do for your boss.

Shukhov went up with Kilgas. They could hear

Senka coming up the ladder after them. He'd gotten the idea, deaf as he was.

The walls for the second story had only just been started. Three rows of bricks all around and a little higher in places. This was the quickest part of the job—from knee level up to your chest and no need to stand on scaffolds.

The scaffolds had all been carted off by the other prisoners—either taken away to other buildings or burned—just so nobody else could have them. Now, to do a decent job, they'd have to make new ones the next day. If not they'd be stymied.

You could see a lot from the top of the plant—the whole compound covered with snow and not a soul in sight (the prisoners were all under cover, trying to get warm before the whistle blew), the black watchtowers, and the pointed poles with barbed wire. You couldn't see the wire if you looked into the sun, only if you looked away from it. It was shining bright and your eyes couldn't stand the light.

And close by, you could see the steam engine that made the power. It was smoking like hell and making the sky black. Then it started breathing hard. It always wheezed like a sick man before it sounded the whistle. There it came now. They hadn't put in that much overtime after all.

"Hey, Stakhanovite! Hurry up with that plumb line!" Kilgas tried to hustle him.

"Look at all that ice on your part of the wall!"

Shukhov jeered back at him. "Do you think you can clear it off by the evening? That trowel won't be much good to you if you don't!"

They were going to lay the walls they'd settled on in the morning, but then the boss shouted up at them:

"Hey there! We'll work two to a wall so the mortar doesn't freeze in the hods. You take Senka on your wall, Shukhov, and I'll work with Kilgas. Meanwhile Pavlo'll clean off Kilgas' wall for me."

Shukhov and Kilgas looked at each other. He was right. It would be easier like that. They grabbed their picks.

Shukhov no longer saw the view with the glare of sun on the snow. And he didn't see the prisoners leaving their shelters either and fanning out over the compound, some to finish digging holes started in the morning and others to put up the rafters on the roofs of the workshops. All he saw now was the wall in front of him—from the left-hand corner where it was waist-high to the right-hand corner where it joined up with Kilgas'. He showed Senka where to hack off the ice and he hacked away at it himself for all he was worth with the head and blade of his pick, so that chips of ice were flying all around and in his face too. He was doing a good job and he was fast, but his mind wasn't on it. In his mind, he could see the wall under the ice, the outside wall of the power plant that was two bricks thick. He didn't know the man who'd worked on it in his place before. But that guy sure didn't know his job. He'd messed it up. Shukhov was now getting used to the wall like it was his own. One brick was too far in, and he'd have to lay three rows all over again to make it flush and also lay the mortar on thicker. Then in another spot the wall was bulging out a little, and he'd have to make that flush too. He figured how he'd split up the wall. The part he'd lay himself from the beginning, on the left, and what Senka'd lay as far as Kilgas, to the right. There on the corner, he guessed, Kilgas wouldn't be able to hold back and he'd do some of Senka's job for him so it would be a little easier on Senka. And while they were busy at the corner, he'd put up more than half the wall here so they wouldn't get behind. And he figured out how many bricks he'd lay where. The minute they started bringing bricks up, he grabbed hold of Alyoshka: "Bring 'em over to me! Put 'em right over here!"

Senka was hacking off the last of the ice, and Shukhov picked up a wire brush and started scrubbing the wall with it all over. He cleaned the top layer of bricks till they were a light gray color like dirty snow and got the ice out of the grooves. While he was still busy with his brush Tyurin came up and set his yardstick up at the corner. Shukhov and Kilgas had put theirs up a long time ago.

"Hey!" Pavlo shouted from down below. "Anybody still alive up there? Here we come with the mortar!"

Shukhov got in a sweat. He hadn't put up his leveling string yet. He figured he'd put it high enough for three rows at once, and some to spare. And to make things easier for Senka, he took part of the outside row and left him a little of the inside. While he was putting up the string, he told Senka with words and signs where to start laying. He got it, deaf as he was. He bit his lips and squinted over at the boss's wall as if to say, "We'll show 'em. We'll keep up with 'em." And he laughed.

Now they were bringing the mortar up the ladder. There'd be eight men on the job, working in twos. The boss told them not to put troughs with mortar near the bricklayers—the mortar'd only freeze before they got to use it—but to have the stuff brought up to them in the hods so they could take it out right away, two at a time, and slap it on the wall. And so the guys who brought up the hods wouldn't stand around freezing up here on top, they'd carry bricks over to the layers. And when their hods were empty, the next two came up from down below without wasting any time, and the first two went down again. Then they thawed out their hod by the stove to get the frozen mortar off it and try to get as warm as they could themselves.

Two hods came up together, one for Kilgas' wall

and the other for Shukhov's. The mortar was steaming in the freezing cold, though there wasn't much warmth in it. When you slapped it on the wall with your trowel you had to work quick so it wouldn't freeze. If it did, you couldn't get it off again, either with your trowel or the back of your gavel, and if you laid a brick a little out of place it froze to the spot and stuck there. Then the only thing to do was pry it off with the back of the pick and hack the mortar away again.

But Shukhov never made a mistake. His bricks were always right in line. If one of them was broken or had a fault, Shukhov spotted it right off the bat and found the place on the wall where it would fit.

He'd scoop up some steaming mortar with his trowel, throw it on, and remember how the groove of the brick ran so he'd get the next one on dead center. He always put on just enough mortar for each brick. Then he'd pick up a brick out of the pile, but with great care so he wouldn't get a hole in his mitten—they were pretty rough, these bricks. Then he'd level off the mortar with a trowel and drop the brick on top. He had to even it out fast and tap it in place with his trowel if it wasn't right, so the outside wall would be straight as a die and the bricks level both crossways and lengthways, and then they froze in place. If any mortar was squeezed out from under a brick, you had to scrape it off with the edge of your trowel fast as you could and throw it away (in summer you could use it for the next brick, but not in this weather). This could happen when you had a brick with a piece broken off the end, so you had to lay on a lot more mortar to fill in. You couldn't just lay a brick like that, but you had to slide it up to the next one, and that's when you'd get this extra mortar running out.

He was hard at work now. Once he ironed out the snags left by the guy who'd worked here before and laid a couple of rows of his own, it'd be easy going. But right now he had to watch things like a hawk.

He was working like crazy on the outside row to meet Senka halfway. Now Senka was getting closer to Shukhov. He'd started together with the boss at the corner, but the boss was now going the other way. Shukhov signaled the fellows carrying the hods to bring the stuff up to him on the double. He was so busy he didn't have time to wipe his nose.

When he and Senka came together, they started taking mortar out of the same hod. There wasn't enough to go around.

"Mortar!" Shukhov yelled over the wall.

"Here she comes!" Pavlo shouted back.

Another hod came along, and they used up what was still soft. But a lot of it was frozen to the sides and they told the fellows to scrape it off themselves.

There was no sense in them carrying all the frozen stuff down again.

"Okay, that's it. Next one."

Shukhov and the other bricklayers didn't feel the cold any more. They were now going all out and they were hot—the way you are at the start of a job like this when you get soaking wet under your coat and jacket and both shirts. But they didn't stop for a second and went on working like crazy. After an hour, they got so hot the sweat dried on them. The main thing was they didn't get the cold in their feet. Nothing else mattered. The slight cutting wind didn't take their minds off the work. Only Klevshin kept banging one foot against the other. He wore size nine, but each boot was a different size and both were tight.

Tyurin kept shouting for more mortar and so did Shukhov. Any fellow who really worked hard always became a sort of gang boss for a time. The main thing for Shukhov was not to lag behind, and for this he'd have chased his own brother up and down that ladder with a hod.

At first it was the Captain and Fetyukov who carried the stuff up together. The ladder was steep and slippery, and for a time the Captain went pretty slow. Shukhov tried to push him a little: "Come on there, Captain. We need more bricks, Captain."

But the Captain got better all the time and Fetyukov got slacker and slacker. He kept tilting the hod—

the sonofabitch—and spilled some of the mortar to ease the load.

Once Shukhov gave him a poke in the back. "You lazy slob. I bet you really took it out on the fellows in that factory you managed!"

"Boss," the Captain shouted, "give me a man to work with. I can't go on with this shithead."

So Tyurin switched them around. He put Fetyukov on the job throwing bricks up to the scaffold in a place where they could see how much work he was doing. And he put Alyoshka with the Captain. Alyoshka was a quiet fellow and he took orders from anybody who felt like giving them. "Full steam ahead, sailor," the Captain shouted at him. "Look at the way they're laying those bricks."

Alyoshka gave him that meek smile of his. "If we have to go faster, then let's go. Whatever you say." And they went down the ladder. A meek fellow like that is a real godsend in any gang.

The boss shouted down to somebody. It seemed another truck with bricks had come. They hadn't brought a brick for six months and now they were coming thick and fast. This was the time to work, while they were still bringing them. It was only the first day. If things got held up later on they'd never get back in the swing of it.

Down below the boss was swearing again, something about the hoist. Shukhov would've liked to find out what was going on, but he didn't have the time. He was finishing off a row. A couple of the hod men came up and told him an electrician had come to fix the motor on the hoist. The foreman in charge of electrical work had come with him. He was a "free" worker and he just stood looking while the electrician tinkered with the motor.

That's how it always was. One fellow looked on while the other worked. If they could fix the hoist now they could use it to bring up the bricks and mortar.

Shukhov was already on his third row of bricks (and so was Kilgas) when another of those higher-ups who were always looking over your shoulder came up the ladder. This was the building foreman, Der. He was from Moscow. They said he'd once worked in a ministry there.

Shukhov was standing close to Kilgas and he jerked his thumb over at Der.

"Aha." Kilgas just shrugged. "I don't have anything to do with that sort, but if he falls off the ladder just call me."

Der would now sneak up behind them and watch them work. Shukhov just couldn't stand these nosy guys. Der was trying to rise in the world and get himself made an engineer, the damn swine. He'd once tried to show them how to lay bricks and Shukhov just laughed himself sick. To his and everybody else's way of thinking, you should build a house with your own hands before you started talking about being an engineer.

In Shukhov's home village there were no stone houses, only wooden shacks. And the school was built of logs too—they got as much wood as they liked from the forest. But now in the camp he had to do a bricklayer's job. So okay, he did. Anybody who knew two trades could pick up a dozen more just like that.

Der didn't fall off the ladder, he only tripped a couple of times. He almost ran up.

"Tyurin," he yelled, and his eyes were popping out of his head. "Tyurin!" Pavlo ran up the ladder after him with his shovel in his hands. Der was wearing a quilted coat like everybody else in the camp, but it was new and clean. He had a good leather cap on his head, but he had a number on it like everybody else—B-731.

"What is it?" Tyurin came up to him with his trowel. His cap had slipped to one side and covered his eye.

Something was up. Shukhov didn't want to miss it, but the mortar was freezing in his hod. He kept right on working while he listened.

"What the hell is this?" Der bawled. He was

foaming at the mouth. "You'll get more than a stretch in the can for this. This is a criminal matter, Tyurin. You'll get another sentence for this on top of the two you already have."

Now it hit Shukhov what it was all about. He shot a glance at Kilgas—he'd already caught on. It was the roofing-felt! Der had seen it on the windows.

Shukhov wasn't a bit worried about himself—his boss wouldn't give him away—but he was scared for Tyurin. The boss was like a father to you, but to *them* he was nothing at all. Up here in the North they were always slapping on new sentences for things like this.

God, the way the boss's face twitched all over. The way he threw his trowel on the floor and went over to Der. Der looked around. Pavlo was standing there with his shovel up.

He hadn't brought it up with him for nothing. . . . And Senka, deaf as he was, had seen what it was all about. And he came out with his hands on his hips. He was strong as an ox. Der started blinking. He was worried and he looked around for a way out. The boss leaned over close to Der and said kind of quiet, but so you could hear it up there: "Times have changed for scum like you, handing out new sentences! If you say a word, you bloodsucker, you won't be alive much longer. Get it?" The boss was shaking all over and he couldn't stop.

And Pavlo was looking murder at Der. He had a face like a hawk.

"Take it easy, boys. Take it easy," Der said. He was all pale and he edged away from the ladder a little.

The boss didn't say another word. He straightened his cap, picked up his bent trowel, and went back to his wall.

And Pavlo went slowly downstairs again with his shovel. Very slowly. . . .

Der was scared to stay up here, and he was scared to go back down the ladder too. He went and stood near Kilgas.

Kilgas laid bricks like a druggist weighing out medicine. He had a face like a doctor and he was never in a rush. He stood with his back to Der like he hadn't seen him.

Der sidled up to the boss. He was singing a different tune now. "What do I say to the work-supervisor, Tyurin?"

The boss went on laying bricks and didn't turn his head: "Tell him—*it was there before*. Say it was here when we came."

Der hung around a little longer. He saw they wouldn't kill him now. He walked up and down with his hands in his pockets.

"Hey, S-854," he growled at Shukhov. "Why you laying that mortar on so thin?"

He had to take it out on somebody. He couldn't

find fault with anything else so he picked on the mortar.

"You might like to know, my dear sir," Shukhov said through that gap in his teeth and leered at him, "if I lay this stuff on thick now, this power plant'll just melt away in the spring."

Der scowled.

"You're a bricklayer and you have to do what your foreman tells you." And he puffed up his cheeks the way he always did. Well, maybe Shukhov was laying it on a little thin in places and it could be a little thicker, but only if you worked in the right weather, not in this freezing cold. They should have a heart, but all they think about is output. But how could you get this across to people who didn't have any brains? Der took his time going down the ladder.

"You fix up that hoist for me," Tyurin shouted after him. "What do you think we are, mules or something, hauling bricks up here by hand?"

"You get a rate for haulage," Der answered from the ladder, but he wasn't shouting any more.

"You mean that crap in the rules and regulations about 'Wheelbarrows, For the Use of'? I'd like to see *you* running a wheelbarrow up that ladder. Give us a rate 'Hods, For the Use of.' "

"You don't think I'd mind, do you? Trouble is, the bookkeeping section wouldn't pass it."

"You and your damn bookkeepers! I've got the whole gang working here just to keep four bricklayers

busy. What's it going to look like on the work sheet?"
He didn't stop laying bricks for a second while he
was saying all this. "Mortar!" he shouted down.

"Mortar!" Shukhov shouted right after him.

They'd finished up the third row of bricks and
they could really get going on the fourth. He ought
to raise the level of the string, but he didn't want
to waste time and he'd manage as it was and do the
next row without it.

Der went off across the compound. He was shiver-
ing and was going to the office to get warm. He
hadn't felt too good up at the power plant. He
should've thought twice before taking on a tough
customer like Tyurin. He could've gotten along fine
with the gang bosses—he didn't have to kill himself
working, he had a big ration and a room to himself,
so what more did he want? He just couldn't help
throwing his weight around and acting smart.

Somebody came up and said the electrician and
the work-supervisor had gone away and hadn't managed to fix up the hoist.

So they just had to go on doing the work of mules.

Shukhov had been on lots of different jobs and it
was always the same story. Machines either broke
down themselves or they were broken by the prisoners. He remembered how they'd broken the con-
veyor belt in the lumber camp. They put a stick in
the works and pressed on it. They wanted a rest. You

had to keep piling those logs on without a break.

"More bricks, more bricks, more bricks!" the boss was yelling, and he told them to go screw their mothers, the whole damn bunch of them, the hod men and the fellows bringing the bricks.

"Pavlo wants to know what to do about the mortar," they shouted up from below.

"How much more do you want?"

"We've still got half a trough down there."

"Well, give us another one."

Things were really moving fast now—they were on the fifth row of bricks. They'd had to bend double for the first one and now the wall was up to their chests. It was easy enough with no windows and no doors—just two solid walls and all the bricks in the world. They should've put the string up higher, but it was too late.

Gopchik spread the word that 82 had gone to hand in their tools. Tyurin looked murder at him. "Get on with the job, you little squirt. Keep those bricks moving."

Shukhov looked around. Yeah, the sun was going down. It was all red and there was a kind of gray haze around it. And just when they'd gotten into stride. They were on the fifth row now and that would be the last today.

The fellows bringing the mortar were winded like horses. The Captain looked kind of gray in the face. He was forty, after all, or thereabout.

It was getting colder all the time. Work or no work, your fingers felt numb already in these thin mittens. And the cold was coming into Shukhov's left boot. He kept stomping it on the floor.

He didn't have to bend down to lay the wall any more, but he had the backbreaking business of bending down for every brick and every scoop of mortar.

"Hey, you guys, hey!" He started badgering the men bringing the bricks and mortar. "Can't you get those bricks over here?"

The Captain would have done it gladly, but he didn't have the strength. He wasn't used to this sort of work. But Alyoshka said, "Okay, Ivan Denisovich, whatever you say."

Alyoshka would never say no. He always did whatever you asked. If only everybody in the world was like that, Shukhov would be that way too. If someone asked you, why not help him out? They were right on that, these people. From way over on the other side of the compound—it came over loud and clear at the power plant—they could hear them pounding the rail. The signal to knock off! They'd made too much mortar. That's what came of trying too hard.

"Mortar! Mortar!" the boss shouted.

They'd just mixed a lot more so they'd have to go on laying now. There was no other way. If they didn't empty the mixer they'd have to smash it up the next morning because the mortar would be hard as iron and they'd never be able to hack it out.

"Come on, keep at it, fellows!" Shukhov was shouting.

Kilgas didn't like this. He didn't like rush jobs but he went on for all he was worth. He couldn't do anything else. Pavlo came running upstairs with a hod on his back and a trowel in his hand. He wanted to help with the bricklaying too, so there were five trowels on the job now.

There wasn't much time to lay bricks in the tough spots. Shukhov always picked out the right brick beforehand. He pushed the gavel over to Alyoshka and told him, "Here, knock it into shape for me."

You can't work well if you're in too much of a hurry. Now that the others were going full blast, Shukhov slowed down and took a good look at the wall. He went to the main corner on the right and sent Senka over to the left-hand one. If there was any trouble with the corners they'd lose a lot of time the next morning.

"Stop!" He grabbed a brick from Pavlo and laid it himself. Then he saw at the other end that Senka was doing the wrong thing at his corner. He dashed over and straightened things out with a couple of bricks.

The Captain trudged up with another hod. He was as willing as an old carthorse.

"Two more to come!" he shouted.

He could barely stand on his feet any more, the Captain, but he kept on going. Shukhov had an old horse like that at home once. He took good care of that old horse, but he worked himself to death. And then they skinned the hide off him.

The sun was really going down now. They didn't need Gopchik to tell them—they could see all the other gangs had handed in their tools and were crowding over to the guardroom. (Nobody ever went over right away after they'd pounded the rail—they weren't crazy enough to stand around there freezing. They stayed put in their shelters. But then after a while the gang bosses would agree among themselves on the right moment for all the gangs to come out together. The prisoners were so pigheaded that otherwise they'd just hang around till midnight, waiting for the others.)

Tyurin got some sense now. He could see how late they were. The fellow in the tool shed must be cursing him like crazy.

"Hey!" he shouted. "Don't worry about all that shit. Who cares about it? Get downstairs and empty out that mixer. Take the stuff and put it in that hole over there and cover it over with snow so nobody can see it. And you, Pavlo, get a couple of other guys, collect all the tools, and turn them in. I'll send the last three trowels over with Gopchik. We'll just finish off these two hods here."

They rushed over and grabbed Shukhov's gavel

out of his hand and took his string down. Then the hod men and the brick carriers beat it down the ladder. There was nothing more for them to do up here. There were just the three bricklayers left—Kilgas, Klevshin, and Shukhov. Tyurin went around and looked at what they'd done. He was pleased. Not bad, eh, for one afternoon's work? And without that fucking hoist too.

Shukhov saw Kilgas still had a little mortar left. He was worried about Tyurin getting hell in the tool shed for not bringing the trowels back on time.

"Listen, boys." Shukhov had a bright idea. "You give yours to Gopchik so he can take 'em over and I'll finish off the job with mine. They don't know I've got it so they won't have to check it in."

The boss laughed. "What the hell are we going to do without you when you've served your time? We'll all be crying our hearts out for you." Shukhov laughed too and then went on with the job. Kilgas went off with the trowels. Senka started passing bricks to Shukhov and put Kilgas' mortar into his hod.

Gopchik ran to the tool shed to try and catch up with Pavlo. And the rest of 104 started off for the guardroom without the boss. True, the boss's word went a long way, but what the escort guards said was law. If they booked you for being late, you could land in the cooler. There was a great crowd around the guardroom. Everybody was there.

From the looks of it the escort had begun counting them.

They counted you twice on the way out—once with the gates still shut, so they knew if they could open them, and then a second time when you were going through the gates. And if they thought there was something wrong, they did a recount outside.

To hell with that mortar. The boss waved his arm. "Dump it over the wall and clear out."

"You better beat it, boss. You're needed over there." And just as a joke, as the boss clumped down the ladder, he said: "Why do the sonsofbitches give us such a short working day? You've just about gotten into the job and they pull you off it!"

Shukhov was on his own with the deaf fellow now. You couldn't talk with him very much, but you didn't have to either. He was smarter than everybody and caught on to everything without having to be told.

Slap on the mortar! Slap on the bricks! Press 'em down and look 'em over! Mortar, brick, mortar, brick. . . .

The boss had said not to worry about the mortar. ("Dump it over the wall and clear out.") But Shukhov was kind of funny about these things. And he couldn't help it even after eight years of camps. He still worried about every little thing and about all kinds of work. He couldn't stand seeing things wasted.

Mortar, brick, mortar, brick. . . .

"That does it," Senka shouted. "Let's get the hell out of here."

He grabbed the hod and went down the ladder. But Shukhov—the guards could set the dogs on him for all he cared now—ran back to have a last look. Not bad. He went up and looked over the wall from left to right. His eye was true as a level. The wall was straight as a die. His hands were still good for something!

He ran down the ladder. Senka was already halfway down the rise.

"Come on, come on," Senka said over his shoulder.

"You go ahead. I'm coming," Shukhov said and waved his hand. And he went back inside. He couldn't leave his trowel just like that. Maybe he wouldn't be on the job tomorrow. Or maybe they'd put the gang on the Socialist Community Development and they wouldn't be here for another six months. He'd never see his trowel again. So he had to stash it away. Both stoves had gone out. It was dark and he felt sort of scared. He wasn't scared about the dark itself but because he was here alone. And he'd be missed at the checkout and the guards might beat him up.

All the same he took a close look around till he found a rock in the corner. He rolled it back, put the trowel under it, and covered it up. Now everything was okay!

All he had left to do was catch up with Senka fast as he could. But Senka'd only gone a few yards and was waiting for him. He wasn't the kind to leave you in the lurch. If you were in trouble, he was always there to take the rap with you.

The two of them ran off together. Senka was taller than Shukhov by half a head, and he had a great big head at that.

There are some people with nothing better to do than race each other around a track just for sport and of their own free will. How would they like it, the bastards, if they had to do it after a real day's work, without a chance to straighten their backs, with their mittens soaked in sweat, and their boots worn all thin—and in freezing cold like this?

They were panting like hell.

But the boss was over there at the guardroom and he'd think of something to tell them.

Now they were almost back with the others, and it frightened them.

A hundred voices bawled at them: "Scum! Bastards! Motherfuckers ... !" It's a terrible thing when hundreds of men start shouting at you all at once. What really bothered them was what would the escort guards do to them?

But it looked like the guards didn't give a damn.

Tyurin was here at the back of the crowd. He'd told them and taken the blame on himself.

The men were still screaming murder. They were screaming so even Senka, deaf as he was, could hear it. And he got so mad he started shouting back. He was a quiet sort of fellow but now he laced into them. He shook his fist and he looked like he'd go for them. And then the men quieted down and some of them laughed.

"Hey, 104," somebody shouted. "We thought that guy of yours was deaf. We were only checking up." They all laughed, even the escorts.

"Line up by fives!"

They didn't open the gates. They weren't sure everything was all right yet. And they shoved the crowd back (they'd all pushed up to the gate, the dopes, as if that'd get 'em out sooner).

"Line up by fi-i-ves!"

And they started moving forward by fives, a few yards at a time, as they were called.

Shukhov had gotten his breath back now and he looked up at the sky. The moon had come up full and it looked all purple, and maybe it was on the wane already. It had been much higher up this time the day before.

Shukhov was glad they'd gotten off so easy, and he poked the Captain in the ribs, sort of kidding him. "Captain, tell me what it says in those books you've studied about what happens to the old moon when it goes down."

"What d'you mean? Where does it go? You're just ignorant. It's simply you can't see it!"

Shukhov shook his head and laughed. "But if you can't see it, how do you know it's there?"

"So you think"—the Captain just looked at him— "so you think we get a brand-new moon every month?"

"Well, don't we? If people are born every day, why shouldn't there be a brand-new moon every four weeks?"

"Come off it." The Captain spat. "I've never met such a dumb sailor in my life. Where d'you think the old one goes to?"

"Well, that's what I'm asking you," Shukhov said, and you could see the gap in his teeth.

"Well, you tell me."

Shukhov sighed and said with that funny lisp of his: "The old people at home used to say God breaks the old moon up into stars."

"What ignorance," the Captain said and laughed. "Never heard that one before. Do you believe in God then, Shukhov?"

"And why not?" Shukhov said. "When He thunders up there in the sky, how can you help believe in Him?"

"And why does God do that?"

"Do what?"

"Break the moon up into stars," the Captain said.

"Don't you see?" And Shukhov shrugged his shoulders. "The stars keep falling down, so you've got to have new ones in their place."

"Get a move on there, you motherfuckers!" the guards yelled. "Line up!"

They were being counted now. The Captain and Shukhov were the last in line.

The escort guards got worried and looked at the board they were checking off from. Somebody missing! It wasn't the first time. If they could only count!

By their count it was four hundred and sixty-two, but they had an idea there ought to be four hundred and sixty-three. They pushed the men back from the gates (they'd crowded up to them again). And now it started all over: "Line up by fives! One, two . . . !" The worst thing about these recounts was it cut into *your* time, not *theirs*. And you still had to walk those two miles back to the camp and line up in front of the friskers before they let you in. So everybody from all the sites was in one hell of a hurry to get back and make it inside the camp before anybody else. The first ones inside had a head start—they were first in the mess hall, first to get their packages if they had any, first into the kitchen to get the stuff they'd asked to have cooked in the morning, first to the

CES to pick up letters from home, first to the censors to hand in a letter for mailing, first to the barbers, the medics, and the bathhouse—in fact, first everywhere.

And the escorts weren't sorry to see the last of them and hand them over at the camp. It was no fun for them either. They had a lot to do and not much time for themselves.

They'd gotten mixed up in the count again. Shukhov thought when they started letting them through by fives there'd be three in the last row, but no, it was two again. The fellows keeping count went up to the chief of the escort with their boards and talked it over.

The chief shouted: "Boss of 104!"

Tyurin moved up half a step: "Here!"

"Do you have anybody on at the power plant still? Think!"

"No."

"Use your brains or I'll beat 'em out."

"No, I say."

But he looked sideways at Pavlo. Maybe somebody'd fallen asleep in the power plant.

"Line up by gangs!" the chief of the escort shouted. But they were standing by fives, all mixed up and not by gangs. Now they started shoving into each other and shouting: "Over here, 76!" "Here I am, 13!" "This way, 32!"

Gang 104 was right at the end of the line and they formed up there. Shukhov saw most of them had nothing in their hands. They'd been so busy they hadn't picked up any pieces of wood, the crazy bastards. Only two of them had small bundles.

It was the same game every day. Before the signal to knock off the men picked up scraps of wood, sticks, and broken laths and tied them up with a piece of rag or worn-out rope to take back to camp. First they frisked you for it by the guardroom coming out—either the work-supervisor or a foreman. If one of them was standing there they told you to throw it on the ground (they'd already sent millions of rubles up the chimney and they thought they could make up for it with these splinters of wood).

But what the prisoners figured was if every man from every gang brought just one little piece back with him, it'd be that much warmer in the barracks. Because the orderlies only brought in ten pounds of coal dust for each stove and you didn't get much warmth from that. So what they did was break these pieces up or saw them short as they could and stick them under their coats. To get past the work-supervisor.

The escort guards never told you to throw this

firewood down out here on the site. They needed
firewood too, but they couldn't carry it themselves.
For one thing, they weren't supposed to in uniform,
and for another, they were holding their tommy
guns with both hands to shoot at the prisoners if they
had to. But once they got them back to camp it was
a different story and they gave the order: "Row
Such-and-Such to Row Such-and-Such, drop your
wood here!" But they had a heart. They had to
leave some for the warders and even some for the
prisoners or there'd be none at all for anybody.

So what happened was every prisoner carried
wood every day but you never knew if you'd get it
through or when they'd take it away from you.

At the same time Shukhov was looking around the
place to see if there was anything to pick up, the
boss counted them all and said to the chief escort:
"104 all here."

Caesar'd left the fellows in the office too and
come over. You could see the red light from the pipe
he was puffing away at and his mustache was all
white with frost. He asked the Captain: "Well,
how're things, Captain?"

A guy who's warm doesn't know what it's like to
be frozen or he wouldn't ask stupid questions like
that.

The Captain shrugged his shoulders and said:
"How're things, you say? Well, I've broken my

back with work and I can hardly stand up straight."

What he wanted to say was: "Don't you see I want a smoke?"

And Caesar gave him some tobacco. The Captain was the only man in the gang he tried to stay friends with. There was nobody else around he could have a heart-to-heart talk with now and then.

Now everybody started shouting: "Man missing in 32! In 32!"

The assistant gang boss from 32 and another fellow shot off to look in the repair shop. The men in the crowd were asking who it was and what it was all about. Shukhov heard it was that short dark Moldavian. Which one of them did they mean? The one they said was a Romanian spy, a *real* one?

There were five spies in every gang. But it was all phony. It said they were spies in their records but it was just they'd been POW's. Shukhov was that kind of spy.

But the Moldavian was a real one. The chief of the escort looked at his list and his face turned black. If a spy'd gotten away he'd really be in for it. Shukhov and the whole crowd got mad too. Who did he think he was, this goddamn skunk, the son-ofabitch, the fucking bastard! It was dark already and the moon was up, the stars were out, and the night cold was getting fiercer, and now this sonofabitch had to go and get lost. Was the working day too short for him, the fucker, with only eleven hours from dawn to sundown? Maybe the judge'd give him a little more!

Even Shukhov thought it was funny for somebody to go on working like that and not hear the signal to knock off.

He'd clean forgot how he'd kept on working himself a little while back and gotten mad because people were going over to the guardroom too early, but now he was standing there freezing and bitching along with the others. And if that Moldavian kept them hanging around here another half-hour, he thought, and the escorts handed him over to the crowd, they'd tear the goddamn bastard to pieces like wolves.

The cold was getting into them now. Nobody could stand still. They stomped their feet on the ground or edged back and forth.

Some guys were asking if the Moldavian could've gotten away. If he'd beat it in the daytime it was one thing, but if he was hiding out now and waiting for the guards to leave the watchtowers he had another guess coming—they'd never leave without him. If there was no mark under the wires to show where he'd gotten away they'd search the compound for three days and keep the fellows up there on the watchtowers till they found him. For a whole week if need be. That was the rule and every old camp hand knew it. If anybody got out it was hell on the guards and they were kept on the go without food or sleep. It made 'em so mad they often didn't bring the fellow back alive.

Caesar was telling the Captain: "Well, you remember that scene with those eyeglasses hanging up there on the rigging,* don't you?"

"Mmmm ye-es," the Captain said—he was smoking Caesar's tobacco.

"Or the scene with that baby carriage coming slowly, slowly down the steps?"

"But it gives you a cockeyed idea of life in the navy."

"But the trouble is we're rather spoiled by modern close-up techniques."

"Yes, those maggots crawling in the meat were as big as earthworms. They couldn't really have been that size, could they?"

"But you can't do that sort of thing small-scale on film."

"If they brought that kind of meat to the camp, I can tell you, and put it in the caldron instead of that rotten fish we get, I bet we'd . . ."

The prisoners started screaming: "Yaaaaah!"

They saw three shapes coming out of the repair shop. So they'd gotten the Moldavian.

* TRANSLATORS' NOTE: The discussion that follows is about Eisenstein's classic film *Potemkin*.

135

"Uuuuuh!" The crowd at the gates booed.

And when they got a little closer:

"Bastard, crock, shit-head, no-good sonofabitch!"
And Shukhov joined in too.

It was no joke robbing five hundred men of half
an hour.

The Moldavian came out with his head hanging
down and he looked smaller than a mouse.

"Halt!" one of the guards shouted and started
writing in his book. "K-406, where've *you* been?"

The sergeant came over to him and he was twist-
ing the butt of his rifle. Some of the crowd went on
yelling: "Craphead, son of a whore, stinking bastard!" But some shut up when they saw the sergeant
toying with his rifle.

The Moldavian stood there with his head down
and said nothing. He sort of backed away from the
guard.

The assistant boss of 32 came up front and said:
"The bastard was up there on the scaffold for the
plasterers. He went up there to get away from me
and he got warm and fell asleep." And he rammed
his fist into the back of the fellow's neck. He let him
have it real good. That was just to get him clear of
the guard.

The Moldavian staggered and a Hungarian from
32 shot over and kicked him in the ass.

This was a lot tougher than spying. Any fool could

be a spy. Spying was all right. It was a nice clean game and real fun, not like slaving away in a penal camp for ten years.

The guard lowered his rifle and the chief of the escort bawled out: "Get away from those gates. Line up by fi-i-ves!"

So they were going to do another count, the dirty dogs. What was the point of making another count? Everything was clear as it was. The prisoners groaned. They forgot about the Moldavian now and all their hate turned on the escorts. They wouldn't back away from the gates.

"What's all this about?" the chief escort screamed. "D'you want to sit on your asses in the snow? That's where I'll put you if you like and that's where I'll keep you till morning!" And he sure would. He wouldn't think twice about it if he wanted. It'd happened plenty of times before and sometimes they had to go down on their knees with the guards pointing their guns at the ready. The prisoners knew all about that sort of thing so they started backing away from the gates. "Get back! Get back!" the guard shouted to get them moving quicker.

"Yeah! Why're you bunching up at the gates like that, bastards?" the fellows at the back shouted. They were sore at the ones up front. So what else could they do?

"Line up by fi-i-ves!"

The moon was really shining bright. It wasn't purple any more and it was way up by now. They'd lost their evening! That damn Moldavian, those damn guards. What a rotten lousy life!

The fellows up front were standing on their toes and looking back to see who'd been missed in the count and if the last row had two or three. Right now their lives depended on it.

It looked to Shukhov like there were four fellows in the back row. He got limp all over he was so scared. Now there was one too many so they'd start the count from scratch again. It was that scavenger Fetyukov who'd gotten out of his own line of five to scrounge the butt of the Captain's cigarette and didn't get back in time. So that's why he was there looking sort of out of place.

The second-in-charge of the escort gave him a clout on the neck. It was the best thing he ever did in his life. And now there were only three men back there. The number was right now, thank God.

"Get away from the gates!" the guards yelled again.

But the men didn't grumble this time. They could see the soldiers coming out of the guardroom on the other side of the gate and ringing off the ground outside.

Which meant they were getting ready to let them through.

There was no sign of the work-supervisor or his foremen—they were "free" workers. So they might get their firewood through this check.

They opened the gates wide and the chief escort was standing outside by the wooden railings with another fellow who had to doublecheck.

"First, second, third . . . !" he yelled.

If the count came out right this time they'd take the sentries off the watchtowers.

They had a hell of a long way to walk back over the compound from those towers. And they didn't phone and tell them to come down till the last prisoner was out. If you got an escort chief with any brains he'd start marching you back to the camp right away because he knew the prisoners couldn't make a run for it now and the fellows from the watchtowers would catch up with them. But if the chief on duty was a dope he always waited because he was scared he wouldn't have enough men to deal with the prisoners. Today's guy was that kind of blockhead, and he waited.

The prisoners had been out in the cold all day and they were so frozen they were ready to drop.

They'd been waiting around like this a whole hour now but it wasn't so much the cold that got 'em. What really made them sore was the thought of that lost evening. There'd be no time for all those things they wanted to do back in camp.

Somebody was asking the Captain in the row next to Shukhov: "How come you know so much about life in the British Navy?"

"Well, you see, I spent a whole month almost on a British cruiser, had a cabin to myself there. I was on convoys as a liaison officer. Then after the war some British admiral who should've had more sense sent me a little souvenir with an inscription that said: 'In gratitude.' I was really shocked and I cursed like hell, so now I'm inside with all the others. It's not much fun sitting here with this Bendera bunch."

It looked sort of eerie all over, with the bare plain, the empty compound, and the moon gleaming on the snow. The guards had already gotten in place —ten paces away from each other and their guns at the ready. There was this black herd of prisoners, and in among them, in a black coat like everybody else, was that man, S-311, who'd worn golden shoulder straps in his time and been pals with a British admiral. And now he had to carry hods with Fetyukov.

There's nothing you can't do to a man. . . .

The escort was all ready and they skipped the "sermon" this time.

"Forward march—and make it snappy!"

The hell they'd make it snappy! They didn't stand

a chance of beating the other columns to camp, so they sure weren't in any hurry. They all had the same idea and they didn't have to tell each other. ("You've kept us waiting around all this time, so now let's see how *you* like it. Bet you're in a hurry to get warm too!")

"Get a move on," the chief escort shouted. "Get a move on, front rank!"

The hell they'd get a move on! They trailed along with their eyes on the ground like they were on their way to a funeral. They didn't have a thing to lose now. They'd be the last back in camp anyway The guards hadn't given *them* a square deal, so let 'em yell their heads off as much as they liked.

The escort chief went on shouting at them for a while but he saw it was no use—they wouldn't go any faster. But he couldn't tell the guards to shoot at them for this—the prisoners were sticking to the law and marching in their column by lines of five. The escort chief didn't have the right to make them go any faster. (In the mornings that's what saved their lives. They went out to the job real slow. Anybody who went fast didn't stand a chance to live out his time in the camp. That way you got too hot before you even started on the job and you wouldn't last long.)

So they took their own sweet time and all you could hear was the snow crunching under their boots. Some of them talked a little, but others didn't bother. Shukhov tried to think what it was had gone wrong in camp this morning. Then it came to him. The sick list! Funny he'd forgot all about it at work.

The medics would be seeing people about now. He could still make it if he skipped supper. But that pain was pretty much gone. He wasn't even sure they'd bother to see if he had a fever. He'd just be wasting his time. He'd gotten over it without the quacks. Those guys could be the death of you.

He forgot all about the medics now and started thinking how to get a little more for supper. What he hoped was Caesar might've gotten a new package from home. There hadn't been one for quite a while and it was high time.

But now all at once something happened in the column, like a wave going through it, and they all got out of step. The column sort of jerked forward and buzzed like a swarm of bees. The fellows in the back—that's where Shukhov was—had to run now to keep up with the men out front.

Shukhov could see what it was all about when the column cleared a rise they'd been passing. Way over on the plain there was another column heading for the camp, right across their path. These fellows must've spotted them too and put a spurt on.

This must be the fellows from the tool factory. There were about three hundred of them. So they'd had lousy luck too and been kept waiting around!

What had happened with them? Sometimes they had to stay on to finish work on some machine or other. But it wasn't so tough for them. They were inside all day and kept warm at least.

Now they'd have to see who'd make it first. They started to run, and the guards ran with them. The escort chief was yelling: "No straggling back there! Bunch up at the back!"

Why the hell was he yelling? Didn't he see they were doing just that?

Everybody forgot what they'd been talking or thinking about. There was only one thing they had their minds on now—get ahead of those other guys and beat 'em to it!

So everything was turned upside down. Everything was all mixed up now—bitter was sweet and sweet was bitter. Even the guards were with them. They were all in it together. The people they hated now were the guys over in that other column.

They all felt better and they weren't half as mad.

"Come on, get going up there!" the fellows in back were shouting.

Their column was now on one of the streets that led into the camp and they'd lost sight of the guys from the tool works behind a housing block on another street. But they were still racing each other.

Now they were in the street. The going was easier and it wasn't so rough underfoot for the guards either. They were bound to beat those others to it!

Another reason they had to get in ahead of that bunch from the tool works—those guys got a real going-over from the friskers and took up the longest time at the guardroom of anybody. It all started with the killing of those stool pigeons—the higher-ups had gotten the idea it was the fellows in the tool works who'd made the knives and brought them in. That's why they frisked them like they did before they let them through. Way back last fall—the ground was getting cold by then—they started yelling at them every time: "Take your boots off, tool works! Hold them up in your hands!"

So they had to stand there in their bare feet for the frisk. And now, in the freezing cold, the guards made 'em take off just one of their boots and they pointed at the one they wanted. "Come on, take off your right boot! And you there, take off the left one!" So they had to hop around on one leg and turn 'em upside down and shake out their foot-cloths to show they didn't have a knife. Shukhov had heard—he didn't know if it was true or not—these fellows from the tool works had brought in a couple of volley-ball posts in the summer and they'd hid all the knives in those posts—ten in each—and knives were still turning up all over the place.

They went past the new recreation hall on the double, past some houses and the carpentry shop, and turned a corner on the stretch that went up to the guardroom. The column let out a great roar like it was one man. This was just the spot they wanted to be, where the two streets came together. The fellows from the tool shop were way behind—five hundred yards down the road. They could let up now. Everybody in the column was on top of the world. It was like a bunch of scared rabbits gloating over another bunch of scared rabbits.

Now they were back at the camp. It was the same as they'd left it in the morning—it was night then and it was night now. There were plenty of lights around the fence but it was nothing to what they had around the guardroom. The place the friskers were waiting for them was light as day.

But before they could get there the second-in-charge of the escort yelled: "Halt!" He handed his gun to a soldier and ran up close to the column (they weren't supposed to come too near the men with their guns). "All those on the right with firewood, throw it over here!"

The fellows on the outside weren't trying to hide it. Little bundles of firewood started flying through the air. Some of them tried to pass the stuff to men in the middle of the column. But these other guys yelled at them: "They'll take it away from everybody else and all because of you! Throw it over there like he tells you!"

Who is the prisoner's worst enemy? The guy next to him. If they didn't fight each other, it'd be another story. . . .

"Forward march!" the second-in-charge shouted. So they went over to the guardroom.

Five streets came together at the guardroom. An hour before they'd all been crowded with the men coming in from the other sites. When all these streets were finished, the main square in the town they were building would be right here by the guardroom where they were going to frisk them. And the people who'd be coming to live in this new town would parade here on the big days, just like the prisoners were pouring in now.

The warders were already at the guardroom warming themselves. They came out and stood across from the prisoners: "Open up your coats and jackets!" And they put their arms out sort of getting ready for the frisk. Same as in the morning.

It wasn't so bad opening up their clothes now. They were nearly home.

That's just what they said—"home." You didn't have any other home to think about when you were out there working.

They were frisking the guys at the front of the column now, and Shukhov went over to Caesar and said: "Caesar Markovich, when we're through, I'll go to the package room right away and hold a place for you in line."

Caesar turned around. The ends of his neat black mustache were all white with frost. Then Caesar said to him: "What's the point in that, Ivan Denisovich? Suppose I don't have any package?"

"Maybe not, but what the hell! I'll hang around for ten minutes and if you don't come I'll go over to the barracks."

What Shukhov had at the back of his mind was—even if Caesar hadn't gotten anything, he could sell his place in the line to some other guy.

It looked like Caesar wanted a package real bad. "Okay, Ivan Denisovich. Go over and get in line. But don't wait more than ten minutes."

They were getting close to the friskers now. Shukhov had nothing to hide from them today and he didn't worry. He took his time undoing his coat and the piece of rope around his jacket.

And though he didn't think he had anything on him he shouldn't, his eight years in camps had made him careful. So he shoved his hand in the pocket on the knee of his pants to make sure it was empty.

And there was the piece of steel he'd picked up on the site! He'd only taken it so it wouldn't go to waste and he didn't mean to bring it back to the camp.

He didn't mean to bring it back—but he had, and

it'd be a great pity to throw it away. He could grind it down into a small knife for mending boots or making clothes.

If he'd meant to smuggle it in he'd have found a good way to hide it. But there were only two rows of men in front of him at the friskers and the first five were there already.

He had to think fast. He could throw it out in the snow while he was still covered by the backs of the men in front (they'd find it later, but they'd never know where it came from) or he could try and get it through.

If they found it on him and said it was a knife, he could get ten days in the can.

But a knife like that could bring something in. It could mean more bread. He couldn't stand throwing it away so he slipped it in one of his mittens.

Now the row of five in front was ordered up to the friskers, so there were just three of them left out there under the bright light—Senka, Shukhov, and the young fellow from 32 who'd helped bring the Moldavian in.

There were only three of them to five warders so Shukhov could play it smart and choose between the two on the right. He picked the old one with gray whiskers instead of the young one with the red cheeks. Of course the old man knew his stuff and would have no trouble finding it if he wanted, but the thing was he was old, so he must be fed up with his job. Then Shukhov took off both mittens, the one with the piece of steel and the other, and held them in one hand (he stuck the empty mitten out a little in front). He put the piece of rope he used for a belt in the same hand, opened his jacket wide, and lifted up the sides of his coat (he'd never put himself out for the friskers like this before but now he wanted to make 'em feel he had nothing to hide). He went up to the old man with the gray whiskers.

The old man ran his hands over Shukhov's back and sides and felt the pocket on his knee and the sides of his coat and jacket, but there was nothing there. To make sure before he let him go, he tried the mitten with nothing in it that Shukhov had stuck under his nose. Shukhov was in a sweat. If this warder did the same with the other one he'd wind up in the cooler with eight ounces of bread a day and hot food only every third day. He thought how weak and hungry he'd be there and how hard it would be to get back on his feet, lean and half-starved as he was.

And he prayed hard as he could: "God in Heaven, help me and keep me out of the can!" All this went through his head when the warder felt the first mitten and then reached out for the one behind it (he'd have tried them both at once if Shukhov hadn't held them in the same hand). But then the chief warder —he wanted to get the thing over with soon as he could—shouted to the guards: "Let's have the fellows from the tool works."

So the old man with the gray whiskers didn't bother with Shukhov's other mitten and waved him through.

Shukhov ran to catch up with the others. They were already lined up by fives between two long wooden rails—like the ones they hitch horses to in marketplaces. It made a kind of paddock. He felt like he was walking on air but he didn't say a prayer of thanks because there wasn't any time and there was no sense in it now.

The guards who'd brought their column in got out of the way to make room for the escorts who were marching the tool works in. They were waiting for their chief. They'd picked up all the firewood the column had thrown down before the frisk. The firewood the warders took was piled up by the guardroom.

The moon was going up higher all the time and the night cold was getting stronger.

On his way to the guardroom to sign in the four hundred and sixty-three men the escort chief stopped and had a word with Pryakha—this was Volkovoy's deputy—and he shouted: "K-460!"

The Moldavian, who'd tried to keep out of sight in the middle of the column, gave a sigh and came up to the rail on the right. He still had his head down and his shoulders were all hunched up.

"Over here!" Pryakha wanted him to come around the other side.

The Moldavian went around. They told him to put his hands behind his back and wait there.

So he was going to get it in the neck for "attempted escape." They'd put him in the can.

Two guards stood on the left and right of the paddock just in front of the gate. These gates were high as three men. They opened them up and then the order came: "Line up by fi-i-ves!" (They didn't have to tell you to get away from the gate here because the gates to the camp always opened in so the prisoners couldn't rush them and break them down.) "One, two, three . . . !"

The prisoners were at their coldest and hungriest when they checked in through these gates in the evening, and their bowl of hot and watery soup without any fat was like rain in a drought. They gulped it down. They cared more for this bowlful than freedom, or for their life in years gone by and years to come. They came back through the gates like soldiers from the wars with a lot of noise and cocky as hell. It was best to keep out of their way.

The orderly from HQ got scared when he saw them come in. Now for the first time since roll call at six-thirty that morning the men were on their own. They went through the big outside gates, through the smaller one inside, across the yard through another pair of rails, and broke loose all over the compound.

All except the gang bosses, who were stopped by a work-controller: "Gang bosses, go to the PPS!"

Shukhov raced past the punishment block and the barracks over to the package room and Caesar strolled over the other way where people were swarming around a post with a plywood board nailed to it. The names of all the people with packages were written up there with a pencil.

They didn't use much paper in the camps. They wrote mostly on these boards. Plywood lasted longer. The work-controllers and the screws used it when they counted heads. They could wipe it clean and write on it again the next day. It was a great saving. There was always some scrounging to be done around this post by people who hadn't been working outside. They'd find out from this board who'd gotten a package, go and meet the fellow at the gate, and tell him the number. You could pick up a cigarette or two like that.

Shukhov ran up to the package room. It was a sort of lean-to with an entryway. The entryway had no door and the cold went right through it, but you were under cover so it wasn't too bleak.

Men were standing in a line all around the wall. Shukhov got in it too. There were fifteen fellows ahead of him so there'd be an hour's wait and that'd take him up to lights out. If anybody else from his bunch had a package—he'd have to go and look at the list first—he'd be way behind Shukhov. So would all the fellows from the tool works. They might have to come back again early in the morning. They stood in line with little bags and sacks and things. Over inside, behind the door (Shukhov hadn't gotten a package since he'd been in this camp, but he knew from what people said), a warder pried open the wooden box with your stuff in it, took it all out and went through it real careful. He cut things up, broke them in pieces, and gave them a good going-over. If it was anything liquid in a glass jar or a can they opened it and poured it out for you. All you could do to try and catch it was cup your hands or get a bag under it. They didn't hand cans or jars over to you. It made 'em kind of jumpy. If there was any pastry or candy or something fancy like that, or any sausage or fish, the warder always bit off a hunk. (And it wasn't worth while kicking up a fuss because then he'd say it was forbidden and you weren't supposed to have it.) Anybody who got a package had to give handouts all along the line, starting with the warder. And when they were through poking around in your package they wouldn't let you have the box —you had to stuff it all into a bag or into the lining of your coat. Then they kicked you out and called the next fellow. They sometimes hustled you so much you left something behind on the counter. And it was no use coming back for it. It wouldn't be there any more.

Back in the Ust-Izhma days Shukhov had gotten packages a couple of times. But he wrote to his wife and told her not to send any more because there wasn't much left by the time it reached him. Better keep it for the kids. Though it was easier for Shukhov to feed his whole family back home than it was just to keep himself alive in the camp, he knew the price they paid for these packages and he knew he couldn't go on taking the bread out of their mouth for ten years. So he'd rather do without.

All the same every time anybody in his gang or in his part of the barracks got a package—and this was nearly every day—he felt a kind of pang inside because it wasn't him. And though he told his wife she must never send him anything, even for Easter, and he never went to that post with the list on it— unless it was to take a look for some other guy who was well off—still he sometimes had the crazy idea somebody might run up to him one day and say: "Shukhov, what are you waiting for? You've got a package!"

But nobody ever did, and he thought about his home village of Temgenyovo and the wooden shack

where they lived. Here he was on the go from reveille to lights out and there was no time for day-
dreaming. He was standing in line with these
people who were keeping their bellies happy with
the hope they'd soon be sinking their teeth into
a chunk of fatback, eating their bread with butter,
and sweetening their tea with sugar. But Shukhov
had only one thing to hope for—he might still
make it to the mess hall with the rest of his gang in
time to eat his gruel before it got cold. It didn't do
you half as much good if it was cold. He figured if
Caesar's name wasn't on the list he'd be back in
the barracks by now and getting cleaned up. But if
Caesar's name was on it he'd now be getting together
bags and plastic mugs to put the stuff in. That's why
Shukhov said he'd wait ten minutes—just to give him
time.

Shukhov picked up some news from the fellows
in the line. There wasn't going to be any Sunday
again this week. They were going to be swindled out
of it. That was nothing new, they'd known it all
along—if there were five Sundays in the month, they
let you off on three and chased you out to work on
the other two. He knew this—but when he heard it
he felt sick all over and it turned his stomach. You
couldn't help feeling bad about losing your Sunday.
Though it was right what the fellows were saying
in the line. Even if you got Sunday off, they still

found jobs for you to do around the camp—putting up a new bathhouse or building a new wall to keep you from getting through somewhere, or clearing up the yard. Then there was always airing the mattresses and shaking them out or delousing the bunks. Or they'd have an "identity parade" to check your puss against your picture. Or they'd say it was time for stock-taking and you had to spread all your junk out in the yard and they kept you hanging around there half the day.

The thing that really got 'em was if the prisoners slept after breakfast.

The line wasn't moving very fast. Three fellows —a camp barber, a bookkeeper, and one of the guys from the CES—pushed up front, and they weren't too polite about it either. These weren't just poor slobs like the rest but high and mighty trusties and the biggest bastards in the camp. To the men's way of thinking they were worse than shit, and they didn't have much use for the men either. There was no sense talking back to them. They all stuck together and they were in good with the warders.

There were ten fellows ahead of Shukhov and seven more in back of him. Now Caesar came along. He had to duck down to get in through the doorway in the new fur cap he'd gotten from home. (That was another thing, these hats. Caesar had given a bribe to somebody in the right place so they let him keep this fancy new cap, the sort they wore in the big cities. But others who'd been brought in with their service caps, straight from the front, had them taken away and got the plain pigskin caps they gave you in the camp.)

Caesar shot a smile at Shukhov and started talking right away with some crazy guy in glasses who was reading a newspaper in the line. "Glad to see you, Pyotr Mikhailovich, old man." And they glowed at each other like a couple of poppies.

The nut with the glasses said: "Look, I've just gotten an *Evening News* fresh from Moscow. It came in the mail."

"You don't say!" And Caesar stuck his nose in the newspaper too. (There wasn't much light from the bulb on the ceiling. How the hell could they read those tiny letters!) "There is a most interesting article here on the opening night of the new Zavadsky."*

These fellows from Moscow can smell each other a long way off and when they get together they kind of sniff at each other like dogs. And they jabber away real fast to see who can say the most words. You didn't hear many real Russian words in all this talk. They might just as well have been Latvians or Romanians.

But Caesar hadn't forgot all his little bags and sacks.

"Caesar Markovich, is it all right if I go now?" Shukhov asked through that gap in his teeth.

"Of course, of course." Caesar lifted his black mustache up from the paper. "But tell me now, who's in front of me and who's behind me in the line?" Shukhov told him where his place was.

And he didn't wait for Caesar to think of it himself but asked him about his supper. "Want me to bring you your supper?" (This meant he'd have to carry it from the mess hall to the barracks in a can. You weren't supposed to. They were very strict about this and kept bringing out rules against it. If they caught you they poured the stuff out on the ground and dragged you off to the cooler. The men went on doing it all the same because anybody who had something to do before supper could never make it on time to the mess hall with his gang.)

When he asked about bringing Caesar's supper over, he was thinking: "You're not going to be stingy now, are you, and not let me have your supper?" They didn't get any mush for supper but only thin gruel.

"No, no." Caesar smiled. "You eat it yourself."

That was all Shukhov was waiting for. He tore out of the package room like a bat out of hell and chased across the compound. There were prisoners wandering around all over the place. One time the Commandant had given an order that prisoners couldn't walk around by themselves but had to be marched everywhere by gangs—except to the medics or the latrines, where they couldn't take them all together. They made up squads of four or five men and put one of them in charge to march them wherever they had to go, wait for them there, and march them back.

There'd been a Commandant who was strict as hell about this order and nobody liked to cross him. The warders jumped on anybody going around by himself and put 'em in the cells. But the whole thing broke down. It didn't happen all at once, it sort of faded out little by little like a lot of these high-sounding orders. Suppose the screws called you out, well, you couldn't go along with a whole bunch. Or you had to go and pick something up in the stores, well, there wasn't much in it for the other fellows to come along with you. Or some guy who got it in his head to go over to the CES and read the newspapers, who the hell did *he* think'd go along with him? And then there were fellows going over to get their felt boots repaired or their things dried out. And then those who just wanted to go from their own barracks to the next one (this was the thing they were real tough on but it wasn't so easy to stop it).

That pot-bellied bastard of a Commandant had made this order to take their last bit of freedom away, but it didn't work out like that.

On his way back Shukhov ran into a warder, took his cap off just to be on the safe side, and ducked into his barracks. There was one hell of a racket inside—somebody's bread ration had been pinched while they were all out at work and everybody was shouting at the orderlies, and the orderlies were shouting back. There was nobody from 104 there.

Shukhov always figured they were in luck if they got back to camp and the mattresses hadn't been turned inside out while they were gone.

He ran to his bunk and started taking his coat off on the way. He threw it up on top and his mittens with the piece of steel too and felt inside his mattress. That hunk of bread was still there! Good thing he'd sewed it in.

So he dashed out again and went to the mess hall.

He slipped across and didn't run into a single warder—just men coming back and quarreling about the rations.

The moonlight in the yard was getting more and more bright. The lights in the camp looked dim and there were black shadows from the barracks. There were four big steps up to the mess hall and they were in the shadow too. There was a little bulb over the door and it was swinging and creaking in the freezing cold. And there was a kind of rainbow around all the lights but it was hard to say if this was from the frost or because they were so dirty.

And the Commandant had another strict rule—
each gang had to march up to the mess hall two by
two. Then the order was—when they got to the steps
they had to line up again by fives and stand there
till the mess-hall orderly let them up.

This was Clubfoot's job and he wouldn't let go of
it for anything in the world. With that limp of his
he'd gotten himself classed as an invalid, the bastard,
but there really wasn't a thing wrong with him. He
had a stick cut from a birch tree and he lashed
out with it from the top of the steps if anybody
tried to go up before he gave the word. But he was
careful who he hit. Clubfoot was sharp-eyed as they
come and he could spot you in the dark from behind.
He never went for anybody who could hit back and
let him have it in the puss. He only beat a fellow
when he was down. He'd let Shukhov have it once.

And this was the kind they called "orderlies," but
if you thought about it they didn't take orders from
anybody. And they were in cahoots with the cook.

Today a lot of gangs must have crowded up at
the same time or maybe they were having trouble
keeping order. The men were all over the steps. There
were three of them up there—Clubfoot, the trusty
who worked under him, and even the fellow in
charge of the mess hall, big as life—and they were
trying to handle things on their own, the crapheads.

The manager of the mess hall was a fat bastard
with a head like a pumpkin and shoulders a yard

wide. He had so much strength he didn't know what to do with it and he bounced up and down like on springs and his hands and legs jerked all the time. His cap was made of white fur soft as down and he didn't have a number on it. There weren't many people "outside" with a cap like that. He had a lamb's-wool jacket and there was a number on it the size of a postage stamp—just big enough to keep Volkovoy happy—but he didn't have a number on his back. He didn't give a damn for anybody and all the men were scared of him. He had a thousand lives in the palm of his hand. Once they'd tried to beat him up but the cooks all rushed out to help him. And a choice bunch of ugly fat-faced bastards they were too.

Shukhov would be in trouble if 104 had gone in already. Clubfoot knew everybody in camp by sight, and when the manager was there he never let anybody through if he wasn't with his own gang. Just for the hell of it. The fellows sometimes climbed the rails going up the steps and got in behind Clubfoot's back. Shukhov had done this too. But you couldn't get away with it when the manager was there. He'd knock you all the way from here to the hospital block.

Shukhov had to get over to the steps fast as he could and see if 104 was still here—everybody looked the same at night in their black coats. But there were so many of them milling around now like they were storming a fortress (what could they do, it was getting close to lights out?) and they pushed their way up those four steps and crowded at the top.

"Stop, you fucking sonsofbitches!" Clubfoot yelled, and hit out at them with his stick. "Get back or I'll bash your heads in!"

"What can *we* do?" those up front yelled. "They're pushing from the back!"

And it was true, the pushing came from the back but the fellows in front weren't really trying to hold them back. They wanted to break through to the mess hall. Then Clubfoot held his stick across his chest to make a kind of barrier. And he threw all his weight behind it. His trusty got his hand on the stick too and helped him push. Even the manager didn't worry about getting his precious hands dirty and took hold of the stick.

They shoved real hard. They had plenty of strength with all that meat they ate. Those up front were pushed back and fell on the men behind. They went down like tenpins.

"Fuck you, Clubfoot!" some of the guys in the crowd shouted. But they made sure they weren't seen. The others kept their mouth shut and just scrambled to their feet fast so's not to get trampled on. And they got the steps cleared.

The manager went back inside and Clubfoot stood on the top step and shouted: "How many times do I have to tell you to line up by fives, you blockheads! I'll let you in when we're good and ready."

Shukhov thought he saw Senka Klevshin's head way up front. He was real glad and started pushing his way through fast. But the men were jammed tight and he couldn't make it.

"Hey, 27!" Clubfoot shouted. "Get moving!" Gang 27 ran up the steps and inside on the double. The rest rushed the steps again and the men in back pushed hard. Shukhov pushed for all he was worth too. The steps were shaking and the bulb over the doorway was making a sort of creaking noise.

"Won't you ever learn, you scum?" Clubfoot was mad as hell. He hit a couple of the fellows on the back and shoulders with his stick and pushed them over on the others.

He cleared the steps again.

Shukhov could see Pavlo go up the steps to Clubfoot. Pavlo'd taken charge of the gang because Tyurin didn't like to get mixed up in this kind of mob.

"Line up by fives, 104!" Pavlo shouted from up there. "Let 'em through, you guys up front!"

The hell they'd let 'em through!

"Hey there, let me through! That's my gang!" Shukhov grabbed hold of the man in front of him. The fellow would have been glad to get out of the way but he was wedged in there too.

The crowd weaved from side to side. They were really killing themselves to get that gruel they had coming.

So Shukhov tried another tack. He clutched the rail going up the steps on the left, pulled himself up by his arms, and swung through to the other side. He hit somebody on the knee with his feet. They kicked back at him and called him every name they could think of. But he'd made it. He stood on the top step and waited there. The other fellows from his gang saw him and stuck out their hands.

The manager looked out from the door and said to Clubfoot: "Let's have another two gangs."

"104!" Clubfoot yelled. "And where d'you think you're going, you bastard!" he said to a fellow from another gang and hit him on the neck with his stick.

"104!" Pavlo shouted after him and started letting his own men through.

Shukhov ran in the mess hall and—he didn't wait for Pavlo to tell him—started to pick up empty trays. The mess hall looked the same as ever—great clouds of steam, and men jammed tight at the tables like corn on a cob or wandering around and trying to push through with trays full of bowls. But Shukhov had gotten used to this in all his years in the camps. He had a sharp eye and right away spotted S-208 carrying a tray with only five bowls on it for one of the other gangs. The tray wasn't full so it meant this was the last time he'd need it.

Shukhov got over to him and said in his ear from behind: "Gimme that tray when you're through, pal."

"But there's another guy over at the hatch waiting for it."

"Let the bastard wait. He should've been sharper."

So they made a deal—S-208 put his bowls on the table and Shukhov snatched the tray. But the other guy ran over and grabbed it by the end. He was smaller than Shukhov. So Shukhov shoved it at him and sent him flying against one of the posts holding up the roof. He put the tray under his arm and dashed over to the hatch. Pavlo was standing in line and he was sore because there were no trays. He was glad to see Shukhov. The assistant gang boss of 27 was just in front of Pavlo at the head of the line. Pavlo gave him a shove.

"Get outa the way! Don't hold things up! I've got trays!" Gopchik the little rascal was lugging one over too. He was laughing.

"I grabbed it while some other guys weren't looking."

Gopchik would go a long way in the camp and make a real old hand. He needed a couple more years to learn all the tricks and grow up and then he'd have it made—like cutting the bread rations in the stores. Or even a bigger job.

Pavlo told Yermolayev to take the other tray—Yermolayev was a big Siberian and he'd gotten ten years for being a POW too—and sent Gopchik to look out for places. Shukhov pushed his tray sideways through a hatch and waited.

"104!" Pavlo called into the hatch. There were five of these hatches—three for dishing out the food, one for men on the sick list (there were ten men with ulcers who got special food, and all the bookkeepers had wangled this diet for themselves too), and the fifth for handing back the bowls. Here the men fought to see who'd get to lick 'em out. These hatches weren't very high up—a little above your waist. All you could see through them was hands with ladles.

The cook had soft white hands but they were damn big and had hair all over them, more like a boxer's than a cook's. He picked up a pencil and checked off from his list on the wall: "104—twenty-four!" Panteleyev was here too. Like hell he'd been sick, that sonofabitch!

The cook picked up a great big ladle and stirred the stuff in the caldron it'd just been filled nearly up to the top. There were clouds of steam coming out of it. Then he picked up another ladle that held one and a half pints—enough for four bowls—and began to dish out. But he didn't dip down very deep. "One, two, three, four . . ." Shukhov watched to see which bowls he filled before the good part settled back on the bottom of the caldron and which had only the watery stuff off the top. He put ten bowls on the tray and went away. Gopchik was waving at him from a place by the second pair of posts. "This way, Ivan Denisovich, over here!"

You had to be careful carrying these bowls. Shukhov watched his step, sort of gliding along so as not to jolt them, and kept shouting all the time: "Hey you, K-920, look where you're going . . . ! Get out of the way, fellow . . . !"

It was tough enough carrying one bowl in that crowd without spilling it, never mind ten. But he got them over to the end of the table Gopchik had cleared off, put the tray down on it real gentle, and didn't spill a drop. *And* he managed to place it so the two best bowls would be on the side he was going to sit at.

Yermolayev brought over another ten. And then Gopchik ran back to the hatch and came back with Pavlo. They were carrying the last four in their hands.

Kilgas brought their bread ration on another tray. Today the ration was according to output. Some got six ounces, others eight. Shukhov got ten. He took his ten (it had a lot of good crust on it) and Caesar's six—from the middle of the loaf. Now the men in their gang were coming from all over the mess hall to get their supper. It was up to them to find a place to sit down and eat it. Shukhov handed out the bowls and kept an eye on who'd gotten one, and guarded his corner of the tray. He put his spoon in one of the two good bowls to stake a claim. Fetyukov took his bowl—he was one of the first—and went off. He figured there wouldn't be good pickings in his own gang and it'd be better to snoop around the mess hall and scavenge—there might be somebody who'd left something. Anytime a guy didn't finish his gruel and pushed the bowl away, others swooped down on it like vultures and tried to grab it—a whole bunch of them sometimes.

Shukhov checked over the helpings with Pavlo and everything looked all right. He pushed one of the good bowls to Pavlo for Tyurin. Pavlo poured it in a flat German army canteen—it was easy to carry it pressed close to his chest under his coat.

They gave up their trays to some other fellows. Pavlo sat down to his double helping, and so did Shukhov. They didn't say another word to each other. These minutes were holy.

Shukhov took off his cap and put it on his knee. He dipped his spoon in both his bowls to see what they were like. It wasn't bad. He found a little bit of fish even. The gruel was always thinner than in the morning—they had to feed you in the morning so you'd work, but in the evening they knew you just flopped down and went to sleep.

He began to eat. He started with the watery stuff on the top and drank it right down. The warmth went through his body and his insides were sort of quivering waiting for that gruel to come down. It was great! This was what a prisoner lived for, this one little moment.

Shukhov didn't have a grudge in the world now—

about how long his sentence was, about how long their day was, about that Sunday they wouldn't get. All he thought now was: "We'll get through! We'll get through it all! And God grant it'll all come to an end."

He drank the watery stuff on the top of the other bowl, poured what was left into the first bowl and scraped it clean with his spoon. It made things easier. He didn't have to worry about the second bowl or keep an eye on it and guard it with his hands.

So he could let his eyes wander a little and look at other bowls around him. The fellow on the left had nothing but water. The way these bastards in the kitchen treated a man! You'd never think they were just prisoners too!

Shukhov started to pick out the cabbage in his bowl. There was only one piece of potato and that turned up in the bowl he got from Caesar. It wasn't much of a potato. It was frostbitten of course, a little hard and on the sweet side. And there was hardly any fish, just a piece of bone here and there without any flesh on it. But every little fishbone and every piece of fin had to be sucked to get all the juice out of it—it was good for you. All this took time but Shukhov was in no hurry now. He'd had a real good day—he'd managed to get an extra helping at noon and for supper too. So he could skip everything else he wanted to do that evening. Nothing else mattered now.

The only thing was he ought to go see the Latvian to get some tobacco. There might not be any left by morning.

Shukhov ate his supper without bread—a double portion and bread on top of it would be too rich. So he'd save the bread. You get no thanks from your belly—it always forgets what you've just done for it and comes begging again the next day.

Shukhov was finishing his gruel and hadn't really bothered to take in who was sitting around him. He didn't have to because he'd eaten his own good share of gruel and wasn't on the lookout for anybody else's.

But all the same he couldn't help seeing a tall old man, Y-81, sit down on the other side of the table when somebody got up. Shukhov knew he was from Gang 64, and in the line at the package room he'd heard it was 64 that had gone to the Socialist Community Development today in place of 104. They'd been there all day out in the cold putting up barbed wire to make a compound for themselves.

Shukhov had been told that this old man'd been in camps and prisons more years than you could count and had never come under any amnesty. When one ten-year stretch was over they slapped on another. Shukhov took a good look at him close up. In the camp you could pick him out among all the men with their bent backs because he was straight as a ramrod. When he sat at the table it looked like he was sitting on something to raise himself up higher. There hadn't been anything to shave off his head for a long time—he'd lost all his hair because of the good life. His eyes didn't shift around the mess hall all the time to see what was going on, and he was staring over Shukhov's head and looking at something nobody else could see. He ate his thin gruel with a worn old wooden spoon, and he took his time. He didn't bend down low over the bowl like all the others did, but brought the spoon up to his mouth. He didn't have a single tooth either top or bottom—he chewed the bread with his hard gums like they were teeth. His face was all worn-out but not like a "goner's"—it was dark and looked like it had been hewed out of stone. And you could tell from his big rough hands with the dirt worked in them he hadn't spent many of his long years doing any of the soft jobs. You could see his mind was set on one thing—never to give in. He didn't put his eight ounces in all the filth on the table like everybody else but laid it on a clean little piece of rag that'd been washed over and over again.

But Shukhov couldn't spend any more time looking at the old man. When he finished eating he licked his spoon and pushed it in the top of his boot. He jammed his cap on his head, got up, took his own bread ration and Caesar's, and went out. You had to leave through another door. There were a couple of orderlies standing there. They had nothing else to do but unlock the door to let people out and then close it after them.

Shukhov came out with a full belly and he felt good. He thought he might look in on the Latvian, though there wasn't much time to go before lights out. So he headed for Barracks 7 and didn't stop off at his own barracks to leave the bread there.

The moon was way up now. It was all white and clear and looked like it had been cut out of the sky. And the sky was clear too and the stars were as bright as could be. The last thing he had time for now was looking at the sky. But he saw one thing— the cold wasn't letting up. Some of the fellows had heard from the "free" workers outside that it'd go down to twenty in the night and forty by morning.

From somewhere outside the camp he could hear the noise of a tractor, and a bulldozer was grinding away on the new road they were building. And every time anybody walked or ran through the camp you could hear the crunch of their felt boots in the snow. There was no wind.

Shukhov would have to pay the same as always for the tobacco—one ruble a mug, though "outside" it cost three rubles, and even more for the better stuff. Prices in the camp were not like anywhere else because you couldn't have money here. Not many people had any and it was very expensive.

In the "Special" camps they didn't pay you a penny (but in Ust-Izhma Shukhov got thirty rubles a month). And if you got any money from home they didn't hand it over to you but put it in an account in your own name, and once a month you could spend something out of this account in the stores for fancy soap, moldy cookies, and "Prima" cigarettes. And you had to write to the Commandant beforehand and tell him what you wanted to buy, and if you didn't like the stuff you could either take it or leave it, and if you didn't take it you could say good-by to your money anyway—they'd already taken it out of your account.

Shukhov got his money by doing odd jobs—making slippers (for two rubles) out of the rags the customer gave you or patching up a jacket (you named the price for the job).

Barracks 7 was not like 9, where he was. His had two big halves, but 7 had a long passageway with ten doors off it, and each gang had a room to itself, seven bunks to a room. And each room had its own latrine and the guy in charge of the barracks had his own cubicle. The artists lived here in their own cubicles too.

Shukhov went into the part where the Latvian was. He was lying on a lower bunk with his feet up on the ledge and he was jabbering in Latvian with the fellow next to him. Shukhov sat down on the edge of the bunk and said hello, and the Latvian said hello but didn't take his legs down. In small rooms like these the men pricked up their ears to see who'd come and what he was after. They both knew this. That's why Shukhov sat there talking about nothing very much. ("How're things?" "Not bad." "Very cold today." "Yes.")

Shukhov waited till the others got back to their talk—about the war in Korea. They were arguing whether there'd be a world war or not now the Chinese had come in.

And then he leaned close to the Latvian: "Got any tobacco?"

"Sure."

"Lemme see."

The Latvian took his feet off the ledge, dropped them on the floor, and sat up. He was real tight-fisted, this Latvian, and when he put the stuff in the plastic mug he was always scared he'd give you one smoke more than you paid for.

He showed Shukhov his pouch and opened it up.

Shukhov took a little tobacco and put it on his hand. He saw it was the same as last time, the same brownish color and the same cut. He held it to his nose and smelled it. Yes, it was the same stuff, but what he said to the Latvian was: "Don't look the same to me."

"Yes it is." The Latvian got mad. "I always have the same. It is always the same."

"Okay," Shukhov said. "Pack that mug for me and I'll have a smoke out of it, and then maybe I'll take another mug."

He said "pack" because this fellow always sprinkled it in sort of loose.

The Latvian got another pouch from under his pillow—it was fatter than the other one. And he took his mug out of the locker. This mug was made of plastic but Shukhov knew just how much it'd hold and that it was as good as something made of glass. And the Latvian started filling it.

"Press it down now, press it down!" And Shukhov poked his finger in to show him how.

"I know how, I know how." The Latvian got mad again and pulled the mug away and pressed down himself—but not so hard. Then he went on filling it.

Meantime Shukhov opened his jacket and found the place in the wadded lining where he kept his two-ruble bill. He eased it along through the wadding till he got to a little hole he'd made in another place and sewed up with two stitches. He pushed the bill this far, pulled out the stitches with his nails, folded the bill lengthways, and took it out of the hole. It was old and limp and didn't rustle any more.

Somebody in the room was yelling: "You think that old bastard in Moscow with the mustache is going to have mercy on *you?* He wouldn't give a damn about his own brother, never mind slobs like you!"

The great thing about a penal camp was you had a hell of a lot of freedom. Back in Ust-Izhma if you said they couldn't get matches "outside" they put you in the can and slapped on another ten years. But here you could yell your head off about anything you liked and the squealers didn't even bother to tell on you. The security fellows couldn't care less.

The only trouble was you didn't have much time to talk about anything.

"Hey, you're putting it in loose," Shukhov grumbled.

"All right, all right." And the Latvian put a little more on top.

Shukhov took his own pouch out of the inside pocket he'd sewed himself and emptied the mugful of tobacco into it.

"Okay," he said. "Give me another mugful." He didn't bother about trying it out beforehand because he didn't want to have his first sweet smoke in a hurry.

He haggled a little more with the Latvian and emptied another mugful into his pouch. He handed over his two rubles, nodded to the Latvian, and left. Then he chased back to his own barracks so he wouldn't miss Caesar when he came back with that package.

But Caesar was already sitting in his lower bunk and gaping at the stuff. He'd spread it all out on his bed and on the locker, but it was a little dark because the light from the bulb on the ceiling was cut off by Shukhov's bunk. Shukhov bent down, got between the Captain's bunk and Caesar's, and handed over the bread ration. "Your bread, Caesar Markovich."

He didn't say, "So you got it," because this would've been hinting about how he stood in line for him and that he had a right to a cut. He knew he had, but even after eight years of hard labor he was still no scavenger and the more time went on, the more he stuck to his guns.

But he wasn't master of his eyes. Like all the others he had the eyes of a hawk, and in a flash they ran over the things Caesar had laid out on the bed and the locker. But though he still hadn't taken the paper off them or opened the bags, Shukhov couldn't help telling by this quick look—and a sniff of the nose—that Caesar had gotten sausage, canned milk, a large smoked fish, fatback, crackers with one kind of smell and cookies with another, and about four pounds of lump sugar. And then there was butter, cigarettes, and pipe tobacco. And that wasn't the end of it.

Shukhov saw all this in the time it took him to say "Your bread, Caesar Markovich."

Caesar was in a real state like he was drunk. (people who got packages were always like this) and he waved the bread away. "You keep it, Ivan Denisovich." Caesar's gruel and now his six ounces of bread—that was a whole extra supper—and this, of course, was as much as he could hope to make on that package. And he stopped thinking right away that he might get any of this fancy stuff and he shut it out of his mind. It was no good aggravating your belly for nothing. He had his own ten ounces of bread and now this ration of Caesar's and then there was that hunk of bread in the mattress. That was more than enough! He'd eat Caesar's right away, get another pound in the morning, and he'd take some off to work with him. That was the way to live! And he'd leave that old ration where it was in the mattress for the time being. Good thing he'd sewed it in—look how that fellow from 75 had his stolen out of the locker, and there wasn't a thing you could do about it.

Some people thought anybody who got packages was well off and fair game, but when you really got down to it, it was gone in no time. And just before a new package came in they were only too glad to pick up an extra bowl of mush and they went around cadging butts. The guy with the package had to give something to his warder, his gang boss, and the trusty in his barracks. They often lost your package and it didn't come up in the list for weeks. When you took it to the storeroom for safekeeping against thieves and on the Commandant's orders—Caesar would be taking his there before roll call in the morning—you had to give the guy in charge there a good cut or he'd nibble his way through it. How could you keep a check on that rat sitting there all day with other people's food? Then you had to pay off people who'd helped you get it, like Shukhov. And if you wanted the guy in the wash house to give you back your own underwear from the wash, you had to let him have a little something too. Then there were those two or three cigarettes for the barber so he'd wipe the razor on a piece of paper and not on your bare knee. And what about the guys in the CES so they'd put your letters aside for you and not lose 'em? Suppose you wanted to wangle a day off and lie around in bed? You couldn't go to the doctor with empty hands. And you had to give something to the fellow next to you in the bunk who shared your locker, like the Captain shared Caesar's. He'd count every little piece you put in your mouth, and even the biggest heel couldn't get out of giving him something.

Some fellows always thought the grass was greener on the other side of the fence. Let them envy other people if they wanted to, but Shukhov knew what life was about. And he was not the kind who thought anybody owed him a living.

He took his boots off and climbed up to his bunk. He got that piece of steel out of his mitten and had a good look at it. He figured he'd look for the right

kind of stone tomorrow to grind it down for a knife
he could use to mend shoes. And in four or five days,
if he worked at it a little mornings and nights, he'd
make himself a pretty good knife with a sharp curved
blade. But meantime he'd have to hide it. He'd push
it between the crosspiece and the boards of his bunk.
And while the Captain wasn't in his bunk down below—he wouldn't have wanted any dirt to fall on the
Captain's face—he pulled the heavy mattress back
(it was stuffed with sawdust, not shavings), and then
he hid the thing there. Alyoshka the Baptist and the
two Estonians could see him doing it from their
bunks. But he didn't have to worry about them.

Fetyukov came through the barracks and he was
crying. He was all hunched up and there was blood
on his lips. So he must've gotten beat up again for
trying to scrounge somebody's bowl. He went past
the whole gang, didn't look at anybody, and didn't
bother hiding his tears. He climbed up to his bunk
and dug his face in his mattress.

You couldn't help feeling sorry for him if you
thought about it. He'd never live out his time in the
camp. He just didn't know how to do things right.

And now the Captain came along in a good mood
with a potful of tea. But it wasn't the kind they got
in the camp. They had two tubs with tea in the
barracks, but who'd call that tea? It was lukewarm
and had the right color, but it was really just slops
and it smelled of rotten wood from the tub. But this

tea was only for poor suckers. Well, the Captain had gotten a fistful of real tea from Caesar and run off to get some boiling water. He looked pleased with himself and set it up on the locker. "I nearly scalded my fingers under the faucet," he said as if he was proud of it.

Caesar was spreading his stuff out on sheets of paper in the bottom bunk. Shukhov could see this through the cracks in the boards, and he put the mattress down again so he wouldn't get upset at the sight of it. But Caesar couldn't do without him.

He stood up and peered over at Shukhov and winked at him. "I say, Shukhov . . . be a good fellow and loan me that 'ten days' of yours, will you?" What he wanted was Shukhov's little penknife (you could get ten days in the cooler if they found something like this on you). Shukhov kept it in the boards under his bunk too. It wasn't half as big as his little finger, but it could cut up a piece of fatback ten inches thick like nobody's business. Shukhov had made this knife himself and always kept it sharp. He stuck his hand under the board again and got it out. Caesar gave him a nod and ducked down out of sight.

You could make something on a knife like that, but it meant the cooler if they found it on you. And if anybody borrowed it from you to cut off some sausage or something he'd have to have a heart of stone if all you got out of it was a kick in the ass.

So now Caesar owed him for this too. After all the business with the bread and the knives, Shukhov pulled out his pouch. He took out as much tobacco as he'd borrowed earlier that day, reached it over to the Estonian in the top bunk across from him, and said "Thanks."

The Estonian spread his lips and sort of smiled at the other Estonian and jabbered something to him. Then they rolled themselves a cigarette out of it just to see what kind of tobacco Shukhov had. It was no worse than theirs, so why not! Shukhov would have lit up himself to try the stuff out, but he could feel from that timekeeper he had inside of him it was getting very near the night check. Before long the warders would be snooping around the barracks. He'd have to go out in the passageway for a smoke, but it was warmer where he was in his bunk. The barracks was pretty cold and that ice was still up there on the roof. It wasn't so bad right now but he'd get frozen through in the night.

Shukhov started breaking off pieces from one of his hunks of bread, but he couldn't help hearing what the Captain and Caesar were saying while they drank their tea.

"Help yourself, Captain, don't wait to be asked! Have some of the smoked fish, and there's some sausage here too!"

"Thank you, I don't mind if I do."

"And put some butter on your bread. Real French bread from Moscow, you know."

"I must say it's hard to believe they still make this sort of bread anywhere. All this luxury reminds me when I was in Archangel once. . . ."

There was a hell of a racket in their part of the barracks—two hundred fellows talking at once—but all the same Shukhov could hear them pound the rail outside. And he was the only one who did. He saw Snubnose, one of the warders, coming in the barracks. He was a stocky little fellow with a red face. He had a piece of paper in his hand and you could see from this and from the way he walked that he hadn't come to catch smokers or to chase everybody out for the check. He was after somebody. He took a look at his piece of paper and asked: "Where's 104?"

"Right here," they told him.

The Estonians hid their cigarettes and waved their hands to get rid of the smoke.

"And where's your boss?"

"What d'you want?" Tyurin said from his bunk and just put one foot down on the floor.

"What's happening about the reports those two guys of yours were supposed to hand in about their extra clothing?"

"They're writing them," Tyurin said and he didn't bat an eye.

"They should've been handed in already."

"The trouble is they can't hardly read or write, so it's not easy." (It was Caesar and the Captain he was talking about! He was a great guy, the boss, he was never at a loss what to say.) "And they've got nothing to write with. There's no pens and no ink either."

"There should be."

"They always take 'em away from us!"

"You better watch what you say or I'll put you in the can," Snubnose said, but he wasn't too mad. "But see you get those reports to the warders' room tomorrow morning! And they should say they've turned in those things they're not supposed to have to the Personal Property Stores. Got it?"

"I get you."

("Looks like the Captain made it," Shukhov said to himself. The Captain hadn't heard what was going on. He was too busy telling his story and eating that sausage.)

"One more thing," the warder said. "Is S-311 here? Is that one of yours?"

"Let me take a look at the list," Tyurin said, just to stall. "How can anybody remember all these damn numbers?" He was playing for time, trying to drag things out till they called the men for the night check, and maybe then the Captain wouldn't have to go to the cooler that night.

But Snubnose shouted out: "Is Buynovsky here?"

"What's that? Yes, I'm here," the Captain called out from his bunk. (Some people move too fast for their own good.)

"Buynovsky? Yeah, that's you all right, S-311. Let's go!"

"Where?"

"You know."

The Captain just gave a sigh and grunted. It must've been easier for him to sail his destroyer on a dark night in the stormy sea than it was to break off talking with his friend now and go to that freezing cell.

"How many days?" he asked and his voice was kind of low.

"Ten! Come on, make it snappy!"

Just then the orderlies started yelling: "All out for the night check! All out for the night check!"

So it meant the warder they'd sent to make the check was in the barracks already. The Captain looked back at his bunk—should he take his coat? But they'd only strip it off in the cells and leave him nothing but his jacket. So he had to go there just as he was. The Captain thought Volkovoy might have let him off, but Volkovoy never let anybody off. So he wasn't ready for this and hadn't managed to hide any tobacco in his jacket. And there was no sense taking it with him in his hands because that's the first thing they'd find when they frisked him.

All the same, Caesar slipped him a couple of cigarettes while he was putting his cap on.

"Well, good-by, fellows." The Captain gave a kind of sheepish look at 104 and he went off with the warder.

Some of them shouted after him: "Keep your chin up! Don't let 'em get you down!" What could you say?

The fellows from 104 had built the place themselves and they knew how it looked—stone walls, a concrete floor, and no window. There was a stove, but that was only enough to melt the ice off the walls and make puddles on the floor. You slept on bare boards and your teeth chattered all night. You got six ounces of bread a day and they only gave you hot gruel every third day.

Ten days! If you had ten days in the cells here and sat them out to the end, it meant you'd be a wreck for the rest of your life. You got TB and you'd never be out of hospitals long as you lived.

And the fellows who did fifteen days were dead and buried.

Long as you were in the barracks you thanked your lucky stars and tried to keep out of the cells.

"Come on, get out!" the trusty in charge of the barracks shouted. "If you're not all out by the time

I count to three I'll take your number and report you to the Comrade Warder!"

This guy was the biggest bastard of them all. He was shut up with them at night in the same barracks but acted like a higher-up and he wasn't scared of anybody. It was the other way around—everybody was scared of him. He could turn you in to the screws or let you have it in the puss. He counted as an invalid because he'd lost one finger in a fight. You could tell from his mug he was a real hood. And that's just what he was. They pulled him in for a real crime, but they hung Article 58/14 on him too. That's why he was in this camp.

And it was no joke. He'd take your number soon as look at you, and give it to the warder. Then you'd land in the cooler for two days with work "as usual."

So people started moving and crowding up to the door, and they jumped off the top bunks looking like bears. Everybody was making for that narrow door.

Shukhov hopped down from his bunk and stuck his feet in his felt boots. He was holding the cigarette he'd just made—he wanted it real bad. But he didn't go right away, because he was sorry for Caesar. It wasn't that he wanted to get something out of Caesar again but he was just sorry for him. He thought a lot of himself, Caesar did, and he didn't know a thing about life—he shouldn't have spent all that time fussing with his package and should've gotten it to the storeroom before night check. He could've eaten the stuff later, but what could he do with it now? If he took that damn bag out with him to the check he'd just make a laughingstock of himself in front of five hundred men, but if he left it here it might be pinched by the first man back. (In Ust-Izhma things were even tougher—the crooks always got back from work first and cleaned out all the lockers.)

Shukhov saw Caesar was all in a sweat, but it was too late. He was stuffing the sausage and fatback in his jacket. He thought maybe he'd carry that along with him even if he couldn't save anything else.

So Shukhov was sorry for him and told him what to do: "Stay here till the last man leaves, Caesar Markovich, and get back in your bunk where it's dark, and don't budge till the warder and the orderlies come through. And then you tell 'em you're sick. I'll go out now and get in the front of the crowd and I'll be the first back. . . ." And he ran off.

He had a hard time shoving his way through the crowd at first (and he had to guard that cigarette in his hand so it wouldn't be crushed). But in the passageway that led off both halfs of the barracks nobody was in a hurry—they were shrewd as hell—and they stuck to the walls like grim death, two deep on both sides, and all they left clear was the outside door. You could only get out of it one at a time and they didn't mind if any dope wanted to. But most of them liked it better inside. They'd been in the cold all day long and nobody was that eager to freeze out there for another ten minutes. If anybody wanted to die, okay, but the rest of them could wait a little.

Most times Shukhov stuck to the wall too, but now he made straight for the door and turned around and smirked at them: "What're you so scared of, you nitwits? Never been out in the cold in Siberia before? Come and warm up under the moon like the wolves. . . . Hey, give me a light, fellow."

He took a light from somebody and went out on the steps. The "wolves' sun," that's what they sometimes called the moon where Shukhov came from.

The moon was real high up now. A little more and it'd be all the way up. The sky was pale—and sort of greenish. The stars were bright and there weren't many of them. The white snow was glistening and the walls of the barracks looked all white too, and the lights in the camp didn't seem very strong now.

There was a great black crowd of men over by another barracks. They were coming out and lining up. And the same outside that other one too. And there wasn't much talk between barracks. All you could hear was snow crunching under people's boots.

Five men came down the steps of Barracks 9, and then another three. Shukhov went in with these three to make up the next row of five. It wasn't so bad standing here when you'd eaten a little bread and had a cigarette in your mouth. The tobacco was all right. The Latvian hadn't lied. It had the right strength and it smelled good.

More men came straggling out the door and there were a couple of rows of fives behind Shukhov now. The fellows coming out were mad as hell at the guys still hugging the walls in the passageway. They had to stand here and freeze till those bastards came out.

The prisoners never got to see a watch or a clock. And what good would it do anyway? They just went by reveille, roll call, the noon meal break, and lights out.

But the night check was around nine o'clock, so it was said. Only it never finished at nine. They always kept you hanging around while they doublechecked, and sometimes it was more than twice. You never got to bed before ten. And reveille, they said, was at five in the morning. No wonder that Moldavian had gone to sleep before the signal to knock off work. If a prisoner found a warm spot any place, he fell asleep right away. They lost so much sleep in the week, they slept like logs in their barracks Sundays. If they weren't chased out to work, that is.

They were all pouring out down the steps now. That trusty and the warder, the motherfuckers, were kicking them in the ass.

The fellows who'd been first in line outside shouted at them: "Thought you were being smart, didn't you, you bastards? Trying to make cream out of shit or something? If you'd gotten out here before, we'd be through already."

They were all outside now. There were four hundred men in a barracks, and that made eighty rows of five lined up one after the other. The rows right in front of the barracks kept their lines of five, but the fellows in back were just bunched up any old way.

"Line up by fives, you at the back!" the trusty yelled down from the steps. But the hell they would, the bastards!

Caesar came out of the door all hunched up and doing his best to look sick. There were two orderlies from the other half of the barracks behind him, and two from their half with some lame fellow. They chased Caesar to the back and lined up in front of all the others. So Shukhov was now in the third row of five.

The warder came out on the steps.

"Line up by fi-i-ves!" he shouted to the men at the back and he had a strong voice.

"Line up by fi-i-ves!" the trusty bawled too. And his voice was even stronger.

But they still didn't line up, the bastards.

The trusty shot down the steps, went to the back, and bawled them out real good. And he punched some of the guys. But he was careful who he did it to. He only hit fellows he knew wouldn't stick up for themselves. They all lined up now and he went back to the steps. And he and the warder started yelling together.

"One, two, three . . ."

Every row of five shot into the barracks when it was called. They were through now for the day!

If they didn't do another check, that is. Any sheepherder could count better than these dopes. Maybe he didn't have any book learning, but he could herd his sheep *and* keep count of them. But these bastards couldn't do it even though they'd been taught how.

Last winter there hadn't been any drying room for their felt boots in this camp and they had to keep them in the barracks all night. They were chased outside anywhere up to four times for a recount. So they didn't bother getting dressed even—they went out with their blankets around them. This year they'd put up drying rooms but they weren't big enough for everybody, so each gang could dry out their boots only two nights out of three. And now when they had recounts they let you stay inside and just chased you from one half of the barracks to the other.

Shukhov wasn't the first to get back to the barracks, but he didn't take his eyes off the fellow who was. He ran right over to Caesar's bunk and sat on it. He pulled off his boots, climbed up on another bunk near the stove, and put them on top of it to dry. It was first come, first served here. Then he went back to Caesar's bunk. He sat there with his legs under him and kept one eye on Caesar's package so no one could pinch it from under the mattress, and his other eye was on that stove so nobody'd push his boots off in the rush to put their own there.

"Hey, you there with the red hair!" he shouted to one fellow. "D'you want that boot in your mug? Put your own boots up there if you like but don't touch other people's!"

The prisoners were pouring back in the barracks. Some fellows in Gang 20 were shouting: "Hand over your boots for the dryer!"

They let these fellows go out of the barracks with the boots and then locked it. And then they'd come running back and hammer on the door: "Comrade Warder, let us in!" But by then the warders would be over in HQ doing their bookkeeping on those plywood boards to see if anybody'd run away.

But Shukhov didn't give a damn about all that today. Caesar was coming back now. "Thank you, Ivan Denisovich," he said.

Shukhov nodded at him and jumped up on his own bunk like a squirrel. He could finish off that bread now or smoke another cigarette or go to sleep if he wanted.

But Shukhov'd had such a good day—he didn't even feel like sleeping, he felt so great.

Making his bed wasn't much trouble—he only had to pull that dark blanket off and flop down on the mattress (he hadn't slept on a sheet since forty-one, it must've been, when he left home, and he wondered why the women bothered so much about sheets—it only meant more washing), put his head on the pillow stuffed with shavings, tuck his feet in the arm of the jacket, and spread his coat on top of the blanket. And that was that, the end of another day! "Thank God," he said.

It wasn't so bad sleeping here and he was glad not to be in the cells.

Shukhov lay down with his head to the window, and Alyoshka was on the other side of the bunk with his head the other way so he got the light from the bulb. He was reading the Gospels again.

Alyoshka'd heard Shukhov thank the Lord and he turned to him. "Look here, Ivan Denisovich, your soul wants to pray to God, so why don't you let it have its way?"

Shukhov looked at Alyoshka and his eyes were narrow. They had a light in them and they were like two candles. And he sighed. "I'll tell you why,

Alyoshka. Because all these prayers are like the complaints we send in to the higher-ups—either they don't get there or they come back to you marked 'Rejected.' "

In front of HQ barracks there were four boxes with seals and one of the security guys came along every month to empty them. A lot of fellows put slips in those boxes and they counted the days—a month or two months—waiting to hear.

Either there was nothing or it was "Rejected."

"The trouble is, Ivan Denisovich, you don't pray hard enough and that's why your prayers don't work out. You must pray unceasing! And if you have faith and tell the mountain to move, it will move."

Shukhov grinned and made himself another cigarette. He got a light from one of the Estonians.

"Don't give me that, Alyoshka. I've never seen a mountain move. But come to think of it, I've never seen a mountain either. And when you and all your Baptists prayed down there in the Caucasus did you ever see a mountain move?"

The poor fellows. All they did was pray to God. And were they in anybody's way? They all got twenty-five years, because that's how it was now—twenty-five years for everybody.

"But we didn't pray for that, Ivan Denisovich," Alyoshka said, and he came up close to Shukhov with his Gospels, right up to his face. "The only thing of this earth the Lord has ordered us to pray for is our daily bread—'Give us this day our daily bread.' "

"You mean that ration we get?" Shukhov said.

But Alyoshka went on and his eyes said more than his words and he put his hand on Ivan's hand.

"Ivan Denisovich, you mustn't pray for somebody to send you a package or for an extra helping of gruel. Things that people set store by are base in the sight of the Lord. You must pray for the things of the spirit so the Lord will take evil things from our hearts. . . ."

"But listen. The priest in our church in Polomnya . . ."

"Don't tell me about that," Alyoshka begged and he winced with pain.

"No. But just listen." And Shukhov bent over to him on his elbow. "The priest is the richest man in our parish in Polomnya. Suppose they ask you to build a roof on a house, your price is thirty rubles for plain people. For the priest it's a hundred. That priest of ours is paying alimony to three women in three towns, and he's living with a fourth. And he's got the bishop under his thumb. You should see the way he holds that fat greasy hand of his out to the bishop. And it doesn't matter how many other priests they send. He always gets rid of 'em. He doesn't want to share the pickings."

"Why are you telling me about this priest? The Orthodox Church has gotten away from the Gospel.

And the reason they don't put them in prison is because they have no true faith."

Shukhov looked straight and hard, and went on smoking. "Alyoshka," he said, and he moved the Baptist's hand away and the smoke from his cigarette went in Alyoshka's face. "I'm not against God, understand. I believe in God, all right. But what I don't believe in is Heaven and Hell. Who d'you think we are, giving us all that stuff about Heaven and Hell? That's the thing I can't take."

Shukhov lay back again and dropped the ash off his cigarette between the bunk and the window, careful so's not to burn the Captain's stuff. He was thinking his own thoughts and didn't hear Alyoshka any more, and he said out loud: "The thing is, you can pray as much as you like but they won't take anything off your sentence and you'll just have to sit it out, every day of it, from reveille to lights out."

"You mustn't pray for that." Alyoshka was horror-struck. "What d'you want your freedom for? What faith you have left will be choked in thorns. Rejoice that you are in prison. Here you can think of your soul. Paul the Apostle said: 'What mean you to weep and to break my heart? for I am ready not to be bound only, but also to die* for the name of the Lord Jesus.'"

---

* TRANSLATORS' NOTE: The words "at Jerusalem," which should appear here, are omitted in the Russian text of the novel (Acts 21:13).

Shukhov looked up at the ceiling and said nothing. He didn't know any longer himself whether he wanted freedom or not. At first he'd wanted it very much and every day he added up how long he still had to go. But then he got fed up with this. And as time went on he understood that they might let you out but they never let you home. And he didn't really know where he'd be better off. At home or in here.

But they wouldn't let him home anyway. . . .

Alyoshka was talking the truth. You could tell by his voice and his eyes he was glad to be in prison.

"Look, Alyoshka," Shukhov said, "it's all right for you. It was Christ told you to come here, and you are here because of Him. But why am *I* here? Because they didn't get ready for the war like they should've in forty-one? Was that *my* fault?"

"Looks like they're not going to check us over again," Kilgas shouted from his bunk.

"Yeah," Shukhov said. "We ought to chalk that up on the chimney. Doesn't happen every day." And he yawned. "Time we got some sleep."

The barracks was quiet and there wasn't a sound. Then they heard the grinding of the bolt on the outside door. The two fellows who'd taken the boots to the drying room ran in from the passageway and shouted: "Second check!"

The warder was right behind them and he yelled: "Get out on the other side of the barracks!"

Some of them were sleeping already. They grumbled and started to move and put their feet in their boots (they never took their pants off, it was too cold under the blanket and you got all stiff without them).

"The bastards!" Shukhov said, but he wasn't too angry because he wasn't sleeping yet.

Caesar reached up and gave him two cookies, two lumps of sugar, and a slice of sausage.

"Thank you, Caesar Markovich." Shukhov leaned over his bunk. "Now you give me that bag and I'll put it under my pillow here." (It wasn't so easy to pinch something from a top bunk. And who'd think of looking in Shukhov's anyway?)

Caesar handed up to him his white bag tied with string. Shukhov put it under his mattress and waited a little till they chased most of the fellows out in the passageway—so he wouldn't have to stand there in his bare feet any longer than he had to.

But the warder snarled at him and said: "Hey, you over there in the corner!"

So Shukhov jumped down on the floor in his bare feet (his boots and foot-cloths were on the stove and they'd gotten nice and warm, and it'd be a shame to take them down). All those slippers he'd made for other people! But never for himself. He didn't mind. He was used to this sort of business and it would soon be over.

And they took these slippers away from you too if they caught you with them in the day.

The gangs who had their boots in the drying room —they didn't mind much either. Some of them had slippers or they went out in their foot-cloths or in their bare feet.

"Get a move on!" the warder yelled.

"Would you like a taste of the stick, you filthy scum?" the trusty said. He was there too.

They were all driven over to the other side of the barracks and the ones who came last had to go out in the passageway. Shukhov stood out there by the wall near the latrine. The floor under his feet was wet and there was a freezing draft from outside.

When they'd gotten them all out from the bunks the warder and the trusty went around and had another look, just to make sure nobody was sleeping in some corner. They were in trouble if they had a man missing, and they were in trouble if they had one too many—it meant they'd have to start checking all over again. They went all around and came back.

"One, two, three, four . . ." They let people back one at a time and it went real fast now. Shukhov was the eighteenth. He shot over to his bunk, put his leg on the ledge, and he was up there in a flash.

It was great! He tucked his legs in the arm of his jacket again and put the blanket and then his coat on top. He'd sleep now. They'd be bringing the guys from the other side of the barracks over here to check them. But that wouldn't worry him.

Caesar came back and Shukhov gave him his bag.

Alyoshka came back too. He was always trying to please people but he never got anything out of it.

"Here, Alyoshka." Shukhov gave him one of the cookies.

Alyoshka smiled. "Thank you, but you haven't got very much yourself."

"Go ahead. Eat it." It was true he didn't have very much but *he* could always earn something. And he put the piece of sausage in his mouth and chewed it and chewed it. The taste of that meat, and the juice that came out of it! He'd eat the rest of the things before roll call, he thought. And he pulled the thin dirty blanket over his face and didn't hear the guys from the other half of the barracks who were crowding around the bunks waiting to be checked.

Shukhov went to sleep, and he was very happy. He'd had a lot of luck today. They hadn't put him in the cooler. The gang hadn't been chased out to work in the Socialist Community Development. He'd finagled an extra bowl of mush at noon. The boss had gotten them good rates for their work. He'd felt good making that wall. They hadn't found that piece of steel in the frisk. Caesar had paid him off in the evening. He'd bought some tobacco. And he'd gotten over that sickness.

Nothing had spoiled the day and it had been almost happy.

There were three thousand six hundred and fifty-three days like this in his sentence, from reveille to lights out.

The three extra ones were because of the leap years. . . .

ABOUT THE AUTHOR

Alexander I. Solzhenitsyn, Nobel prize laureate and Russia's most celebrated living writer, was born December 11, 1918, in Kislovodsk. In February 1945, as a young captain in the Russian army, he was arrested by Soviet counterintelligence, who had discovered in his letters derogatory remarks about Stalin. Solzhenitsyn spent eight years in concentration camps and three years in exile for his offense—an experience that provided the raw material for *One Day in the Life of Ivan Denisovich* and *The First Circle*. In 1954 he underwent radiation therapy for treatment of cancer, which became the catalyst for his novel *Cancer Ward*, published in the late 1960s. In 1962, protected by Khrushchev's anti-Stalin campaign, *One Day in the Life of Ivan Denisovich* was published in the Soviet Union. It remains the only one of his works published in his native land. Solzhenitsyn was awarded the Nobel Prize for literature in 1970 by was unable to attend the Nobel ceremony in Sweden for fear that he would be barred from returning to his family. In 1972, despite government-sponsored ostracism and the loss of most of the privileges afforded other Soviet writers, Solzhenitsyn produced *August 1914* —a masterful account of World War I—and the following year, in defiance of Soviet law, authorized the Western publication of *The Gulag Archipelago, 1918–1956*. This so outraged the Soviet authorities that after waging a campaign of vilification against him, they stripped Solzhenitsyn of his citizenship and on February 13, 1974, expelled him from Russia. He now lives with his family in Vermont and has since published his autobiography, *The Oak and the Calf* (1975), the acclaimed *Lenin in Zurich* (1975), the next two volumes in *The Gulag Archipelago* canon (in 1974 and 1976), a narrative poem *Prussian Nights* (1977), a revision of his Harvard University commencement address entitled *A World Split Apart* (1978), *The Mortal Danger* (1980), *Victory Celebrations* (1983), and the plays *Love Girl and The Innocent* (1970) and *Candle in the Wind* (1974). He was awarded the Templeton prize in 1983.